The Day They Came

by

Gérard L. Breissan

THE DAY THEY CAME is the gripping story of teenager and young adult Gerard's adventures in the South of France and the African Congo. While at scout-camp aged twelve, Gerard meets and forms an unbreakable bond with the alien Eudoxus, who becomes his mentor and guardian angel. Conscripted for military service at the age of nineteen, Gerard later experiences life-threatening danger when participating in a rescue mission in the African Congo. Apart from his own adventures, Gerard also recounts the fisherman Etienne's story about a terrifying and extraordinary storm he experienced in a trawler off Le Grau du Roi in the French Camargue, when six men lost their lives. The story ends when Gerard is twenty-one. Like the writer, whose name he shares, he joins the hospitality industry to see the world. Throughout the narrative and as he grows up and matures, Gerard struggles to remain true to himself, and to find the correct path in life.

In *The Day They Came* Breissan finally speaks out about the many extraordinary events which occurred in his early years, and which he has always felt a compulsion to divulge. It is sometimes difficult to distinguish fact from fiction. You, the reader, must decide which is which.

GERARD LOUIS BREISSAN is a native of Aix-en-Provence, in the South of France; and a Canadian citizen. As a boy, he studied classical literature and showed an early gift for writing, winning many school and regional prizes, as sponsored by the publishers, Hachette and the Lycée Mignet.

He wanted to see the world and chose a career in the hospitality industry as a means of achieving this ambition. He has worked in Bermuda, Canada, the UK, and the USA and has spoken at conferences and given consultancy services in India, the Lebanon, and the Philippines. For four years he was a summer lecturer at the prestigious Cornell University Hotel School, teaching Food and Beverage Management for the professional development programme. While in Canada, he was frequently invited by large food organizations to be a keynote speaker at events such as trade shows and exhibitions at well-known venues which have included, for example, the National Arts Centre, Ottawa. Since 2005, he has been working and living in China, where he is the Head of Hospitality and Tourism Management at Jilin University-Lambton College in Changchun. When possible, he travels around the country to learn about Chinese culture and traditions.

Breissan has always had a passion for writing. While working in London, England at famous hotels such as the Savoy, Connaught, and Hilton Hyde Park Corner, he studied at West London College, subsequently specializing in English writing and poetry. After moving to Canada and rising to executive positions, he continued to write and was in due course appointed National Editor of *Essence* magazine, the official publication of the Canadian Federation of Chefs and Cooks. Food service operators have often used his materials for educational purposes and motivational tools. In 1995, Gérard Breissan received the Sandy Sanderson Journalism award in tribute to his numerous published articles in trade magazines.

The Day They Came

by

Gérard L. Breissan

Proverse Hong Kong

The Day They Came
by Gérard Louis Breissan.
2nd pbk ed. pub. in Hong Kong by Proverse Hong Kong, January 2016
ISBN: 978-988-8228-33-1
Copyright © Proverse Hong Kong, January 2016.
Printed by CreateSpace

1st pub. in pbk in Hong Kong by Proverse Hong Kong, 23 March 2012.
Copyright © Proverse Hong Kong, 23 March 2012.
ISBN 978-988-19934-6-5

Enquiries: Proverse Hong Kong, P. O. Box 259, Tung Chung Post Office, Tung Chung, Lantau Island, NT, Hong Kong   SAR, China.
E-mail: proverse@netvigator.com Web site: www.proversepublishing.com

Proverse Hong Kong
British Library Cataloguing in Publication Data (1st pbk edition)

Breissan, Gerard Louis.
The day they came.
1. Breissan, Gerard Louis--Fiction. 2. Human-alien encounters--Fiction. 3. France, Southern--Fiction.
4. Congo (Democratic Republic)--Fiction.
5. Autobiographical fiction. 6. Young adult fiction.
I. Title
813.6-dc23

ISBN-13: 9789881993465

ADVANCE RESPONSES

Undeniably talented, French-Canadian **Gérard Louis Breissan** has written a fascinating tale about flying saucers and aliens...*The Day They Came*, being undeniably entertaining and always interesting, deserves sky-high marks. – *Cairns Media*, 28 April 2012

"I liked this tale of a teenager's close encounters with an alien who becomes his guardian angel, rescuing him from various scrapes, once in the guise of an ageless Jesuit missionary in the Congo. An imaginative and delightful read, even if you're not a ufologist." – John Russell, SJ, formerly long-time Warden of Ricci Hall, University of Hong Kong.

"Breissan's tale poses many questions for readers puzzled by UFO phenomena. – Alien from another world? Angel from Heaven? Who, or what is the mysterious but benign Eudoxus?" – Margaret Clarke, acclaimed translator of the future fiction classics, *The Last Man* and *The World As It Shall Be* and formerly lecturer in English at Notre Dame College of Education, Glasgow, United Kingdom.

Young Gerard's exploits held my interest from the first page to the last. The fact that the author shares the same name as his character made me wonder if these events really happened to him, or were the product of a very creative imagination. Either way, it was an excellent read, and left me hoping that the author will write a sequel. I definitely want to read more of his adventures. – A. Buchmann (Vancouver, WA, Canada) (First published on Amazon.)

Wow! I love a story that is fun to read AND leaves me feeling good about the world. This story scores on both points. Breissan is a masterful storyteller, able to visually transport the reader from the south of France to the Congo while weaving his tale into the fabric of recent history. If you seek an entertaining and uplifting diversion, read this book.– Steve B. (First published on Amazon.)

Dedicated

to my daughter

Lauren Ashley

AUTHOR'S INTRODUCTION
Gérard Louis Breissan

In this narrative, I have told as accurately as possible about four extraordinary events which marked my life for ever. They took place long ago, but I vividly remember the specific details of their occurrences.

Truly speaking, there has never been any verified proof that UFOs and their occupants have ever landed on Earth. Since 1947 (when sightings started to increase in North America) to this day, the phenomenon of UFOs has rarely been taken seriously.

People who know me well can confirm that I am an upright man, hardworking, an excellent father and that I do not invent stories. I am healthy and right minded.

In this book I will state what I have really seen and experienced and I assert clearly that I am quite certain about the facts that I will write down.

Eudoxus is real and he has intervened in my life a few times over the years without asking for anything in return. When I was twelve years old I was selected as a specimen, but I have never suffered at the hands of aliens. I never flew in space, and implants were never made into my vital organs. My encounters were just that – encounters.

In 2004 I knew that it was time to write my story. I had kept it a secret for too long. As Eudoxus told me the first time we met, "You will know when it is time to tell." I have decided to do it now, before it is too late and all the details fade from my memory.

I am still passionate about ufology. However, after all these years I have come to the conclusion that there are no ufologists. The true experts in the field are people who have experienced real encounters; they are the ones who know the truth and can talk about it. They can tell you why such happenings never leave you and stay in your mind for ever. In my case, it has made me look at life differently and enhanced various beliefs. My own contact is a friend who lives far away. He has unique abilities and because of his interventions I am here today to put it all down on paper.

His name is Eudoxus, and he lives on Toki.

CONTENTS

The Day They Came

CHAPTER ONE
THE SHIP

In the summer of 1959, somewhere near Aix-en-Provence, Southern France, an astonishing chain of events took place that changed my life forever. Father Moyon's decision to move summer camp closer to home was the first of those events.

Father Moyon, the head of our parish, was a very gregarious and active man who enjoyed the outdoors and took it upon himself to help the town's boys "stay out of trouble." Father Moyon's philosophy was simple and straight to the point: "Keep the boys busy at all times, teach them independence, to practice sports, and they will stay on the right side of the law!" I was one of these boys and it worked for me. He was not only a spiritual leader; he also helped the local schools with sporting and social activities. Throughout the year Father Moyon led trips to the countryside but his favourite event was the summer camp.

During the summer camps, boys aged six to fourteen went "outward bound", living in tents, and learned about hiking, mountain-climbing, and how to survive in the woods. In addition, boys had to wash their own clothes, sew their own buttons (if necessary), and help prepare meals. It was quite a life experience and the boys all enjoyed it tremendously.

Summer camp lasted three months and usually took place in the Alps. In 1959, Father Moyon informed us that the summer camp would be moved closer to home for that particular year. I cannot recall exactly what the reasons were for that decision, but it had to do with a very important ecclesiastic convention that Father Moyon had to attend in a foreign country.

My friends and I were twelve years old and excited that we were going to spend an entire vacation camping in Provence. It meant climbing Mont Sainte-Victoire, swimming in the Durance River and, if we were lucky, working in a vineyard for a few days. My friends Richard, Patrick and Jose were going to share a tent with me.

Our holidays started by learning how to set up a camp with large tents called *marabouts*. They could hold thirty to forty people each. After each *marabout* was set up, we dug rain trenches around the perimeter, cleaned the bushes, cut wood for the bonfires and the cooking area, and picked fresh fruits. We bathed and did the laundry in the river nearby. We were very busy all the time, which was of course Father Moyon's objective. That night, we slept like logs.

The weather was fantastic. It was hot and dry, the sky was azure blue and temperatures were reaching 32 to 35°C.

It was paradise for us; however, our daily routine was soon to be interrupted by extraordinary circumstances.

One particular Thursday (I still remember the day), Father Moyon asked Richard, Jose and me to fetch some milk, cream, eggs and fresh tomatoes from the farm nearby.

He had made previous arrangements with local purveyors to supply us with the best products available. In addition, two professional chefs had been hired for the three month period.

We undoubtedly loved the food and did not mind at all the kitchen tasks we were asked to do. We prepared ourselves for the two kilometre walk to the farm where the lady in charge would be waiting for us with some fresh lemonade and watermelon.

It was a very hot day and we decided to take a short cut to a side road across a large lavender field and a corn patch. On the other side of the side road ran a small river. All we had to do was to walk at a fast pace following the stream, then go over a small bridge which led to a sinuous path that would bring us right onto the farm. By taking that route we were saving forty-five minutes.

We were walking briskly, talking, whistling, and enjoying ourselves, not worried about anything. Like all kids our age during a summer camp we were care free.

It must have been noon. All around us the breeze was buzzing with life, as bees, flies, mosquitoes, and butterflies were hovering above the lavender flowers. We started to cross the field and could not stop thinking how lucky we were to be in such a beautiful part of the country, *La Provence*.

Suddenly a piercing noise broke the afternoon's calm. It was a long, strident, shrieking type of sound that came from high above us.

We looked up, and through an opaque illumination we distinguished the dark shape of a flying object. It descended slowly.

We were scared to death. What was it? Where did it come from? Was it going to hurt us? Our first thoughts were: "Martians are attacking the Earth!"

Remember, these were the 1950s. Martians were the enemies! We did not want to look at the descending object, but we simply could not resist doing so. We were witnessing an incredible occurrence.

Not a word was spoken among us.

By looking more carefully through the light and its reverberation, I could distinguish an almost oval outline, more precisely like the shell of a large clam or mussel. It was enormous, perhaps fifteen or even twenty metres in circumference.

The machine came close to the ground, but did not touch it. It started oscillating, left to right, right to left; then stood motionless in the air.

The noise emanating from the object increased to a shrilling, hissing sound, almost unbearable to endure. We covered our ears but it did not help. It felt as if the horrible whistle was penetrating my brain. A green hazy cloud, like a fog, was encircling the craft and a powerful air current coming from underneath was propelling dirt and soil through the air. This frightening device was creating a lot of turbulence. It was awesome.

Patrick, Jose and I were totally flabbergasted.

"What is it?" asked Jose.

"I don't know," I replied. "It looks like a flying-saucer."

"Should I go and get the police?" asked Richard.

I advised against it, just in case the occupants of the machine started shooting at us. I told Richard to wait a little longer to see what their intentions were.

Jose agreed. He was worried that the Martians would use a deadly ray to make us disappear, like in the movies.

The green fumes had now intensified and were blocking the sun from our eyes; in addition, an acrid smell had surged all around the landing zone, which made it very hard to breathe. It smelled like sulphur. All of a sudden, resonant clangs occurred and large powerful white lights turned on. They looked like huge headlights, and were situated all along the middle of the flying-saucer. I could count maybe five or six through the mist.

"There are people in there," said Jose.

"Yes, and they want to kill us," replied Richard.

"Take it easy guys, let's see what happens first, do not move, do not go anywhere!" I said.

I may add that, even though I was scared, I was also mesmerized by what was happening. Was it a dream? It was hard to say.

Another metallic sound; and four large cylindrical tubes slowly extended down from the spaceship. Another clank, and four rotund flat feet appeared. Now the craft was ready for landing. And it did land! It came to rest about two hundred metres from us in the lavender field.

Richard, Jose and I were definitely looking at a real flying-saucer which had arrived from another planet and had berthed in our region of Aix-en-Provence. But who was going to believe us? I may add that, at that stage of the close encounter, no one had stopped on the nearby road; we had not heard any cars honking; we had not seen any boats on the river; nothing. I have never been able to explain why this event took place at lunch time. In France, in those days, people took a three hour lunch break. Everyone was home eating. In addition we were in a remote area in the farming region, close to the hills; it was not a residential district in any sense of the word.

In any case, if anyone had witnessed the landing, they never came forward.

The saucer had landed with a thump. Almost immediately the high-pitched noise stopped, replaced by a humming tone. It sounded as if an engine was running idle.

The heat level had intensified all around the craft. We could feel it from where we stood.

Since no little green man came out of the spaceship, we decided to approach closer. We were afraid, but curiosity took over. We wanted to know who was inside this machine. The monotonous tone of the engine persisted. The large fluorescent lights along the craft dimmed a little, but small probing spotlights – red, green and orange – started to flicker on the top of the saucer. The current of air from underneath the craft suddenly ceased. Metallic clinks followed. A few small vents opened all around the vessel. A resonant turbine buzz combined with a powerful suction noise was activated and almost immediately the green mist dissipated. It was being vacuumed through the openings.

"Wow!" Richard exclaimed.

"It's a big one," Jose shouted.

"It's too bad we didn't bring a camera," I said.

"Yes, because no one will ever believe us," added Richard.

We thought that we heard vehicles on the road, but no one had stopped to watch the landing. The police had not yet been called; therefore, we were the only witnesses to the event. Once the mist had evaporated, the "strange machine" was very visible from where we huddled. On its four legs, it stood approximately eight to ten metres tall and measured 25 to 30 metres in diameter.

It was dark in colour and distinctively made from an unusual type of steel. Somehow, even though the sun was shining right on it, there were no reflections at all. The saucer was built from a dull compound. The humming of the engine was still audible, all the lights were flashing, and we were waiting for some action.

"Let's get closer! I want to see what's happening!" I told Jose and Richard. I could see in their eyes that they were not keen to go further, but without hesitation I jumped up and ran quickly through the lavender field. About twenty metres from the spaceship, I crouched down. Soon afterwards Jose and Richard followed.

From our position in the field and being so close we could distinguish many mechanical features pertaining to the machine that we had not noticed before.

Larger tubes resembling inflated rubber hoses were aligned in parallel under the spaceship's body.

In addition, smaller ducts were entwined in layers. It was quite a sight! Some were red and others were purple. Five or six large exhaust pipes were still producing heat while idling; it was amazing to be part of such an occurrence. The whole scene was somewhat eerie to watch!

We had not surveyed the road and the volume of traffic on it with much attention. I am sure however that several vehicles had driven by without stopping! Did they see what we saw? Were they scared and so just continued to drive? Did anyone call the police? We heard no sirens. No *gendarmes*! We were alone with a spaceship in front of us.

The sun was high in the sky. Butterflies, mosquitoes, and a few bees were flying in front of our faces, and bizarrely this entire scenery was enveloped in the magical scent of lavender. This was Provence, South of France, remember!

"So, what do we do now?" asked Jose.

"We should get the Father down here!" said Richard.

"And do what?" I said. "I want to stay here and watch what's going to happen next. Don't you guys?"

"This thing is unreal, and no one, but no one will believe us," said Jose. "Look, Gerard," he added. The few cars passing by did not even stop!"

They were probably frightened," Richard said.

"Fine, but don't you want to wait?" I argued. "Don't you want to know if there are people in there? Listen, we have sat tight so far without any danger to us. Whoever is in there doesn't seem to want to do us any harm. Let's be patient a little longer. I want to see that machine take off. I really do!"

Neither Jose nor Richard replied, but I knew that they were as curious as I was to learn more about the "flying-saucer"!

"So shall we approach it a little closer?" I asked.

"We'll follow you, Gerard," Jose replied.

We came as close as ten metres from the spacecraft and knelt down in the grass.

All was silent, except for the turbines still running at low speed. The sulphuric smell had been replaced by oil and engine fumes. Now that we were a mere ten metres away from this extraordinary machine, all the intricate details seemed very distinct to me.

I did not want to approach it any further, since from this close I could easily be burned alive by the rockets' flames should the craft decide to take off. I remembered the descent of the saucer into the field and the incredible heat and power it had generated.

I heard again some cars driving by, but no one stopped. They did not even honk their horns. This seemed very strange indeed. If it had been me driving by a field with a large flying object in the middle of it, my first reaction would have been to investigate and definitely call the police. Amazingly, no one seemed to care. What was going on? Why weren't the police here already? Above all, why didn't anyone stop to look? Suddenly, a strident whistle chilled my spine. Immediately it was followed by a loud clang and then another one and then came another strident whistle.

"What now?" I thought.

Jose and Richard were looking at each other not saying a word. We were all scared.

CHAPTER TWO
BLACKED OUT

I looked up, but could not see exactly where these sounds were coming from; the spacecraft was so large that echoes from underneath it resounded everywhere. A vent opened along the front edge followed by a long squeaking noise and to my amazement a step-ladder slowly exited and descended onto the ground. It was built from the same material as the saucer, dark and dull in colour; the steps had hand railings on each side.

"Oh no! Get me out of here!" screamed Jose.

"I'm leaving at once!" Richard said loudly.

"Come on, Gerard. Let's go, before we all get killed!" shouted Jose.

"No, no, please, you guys! Just wait! Why leave now? Nobody will kill us!" I replied.

Actually, I was not really sure about that.

Both Jose and Richard had remained fairly calm throughout this ordeal up to now; yes, we were scared; but a mutual sense of curiosity and strong friendship had kept us motivated and bound together. Undoubtedly, this unique and almost unreal episode would mark us for the rest of our lives. I wanted to hang around to see the end of the episode. I wanted us to be together for the departure of the machine....

If there was ever to be a departure.

However, when Jose and Richard got on their feet and looked at me, I knew that I had to make a choice then and there.

"Are you coming or not?" asked Richard.

"No, I'll stay for a while," I answered.

"Suit yourself, we are getting the hell out of here," yelled Jose.

I could see terror in their eyes and guessed the prospect of facing an alien was too horrifying for them. They had made their decision; I had made mine. I watched them leave as they crossed the lavender field, passed the small bridge and dashed towards the farm. I knew that help would be coming soon. I knew that the flying object was not going to be around much longer.

Now I was alone. I was ten metres away from a large spacecraft and maybe, just maybe, the witness of a close encounter in the south of France.

"What a fantastic story to tell my family and friends!" I thought.

I was standing there, waiting for someone to come down the ladder, but I was not afraid any more. I had analysed the situation and I was ready for whatever would occur.

I could not explain why I wanted to stay right there and watch.

An insatiable appetite for discovering the unknown, combined with an inner force of curiosity, was holding me in the field. Of course there were questions which tickled my brain and for which I had no answers.

"What is going on with the flying-saucer and how long will it stay there?"

"Why isn't anyone coming out yet?"

"Should I run away while I still have a chance?"

"Am I going to die or am I going to be kidnapped?"

"Are the aliens going to make me disappear like in the movies?"

"Where do these aliens come from?"

"Why has the flying object landed in Provence?"

I had too many questions and no answers.

"Forget it, don't worry any more! What will be, will be," I said to myself.

I fixed my attention on the ladder, but I wasn't moving a muscle. Suddenly I felt a knot in my stomach, I was perspiring profusely.

The spacecraft had landed approximately twenty minutes ago. Nobody had stopped on the road. Jose and Richard were hopefully going to send me some help. Father Moyon was probably going to notify the gendarmes. La gendarmerie is the French national body which examines anything pertaining to UFO sightings. They have their own "blue books" and they investigate encounters countrywide. They began monitoring unexplained phenomenon in 1947.

There was no activity from the riverbank. Often in the summer, a few locals and the odd tourist enjoyed fishing in the

Durance; one could catch trout, eel, carp, crayfish, and even salmon.

However, on that day of the encounter I could not see any sails and nobody was fishing.

"My luck again," I muttered.

There was no help in sight and it made me feel uneasy. Where was everybody?

I was still waiting impatiently for someone to come out of the spacecraft. I had a headache, sweat was running down my back and I was disoriented. Suddenly I felt a strange sensation and everything around me seemed to move in slow motion. It was extremely odd. I realized that I was getting butterflies in my stomach, my head was spinning and I was becoming very anxious all at the same time.

I wanted to shout at the flying-saucer, to encourage whoever was inside it to come out immediately.

I yelled out, "Hello, do not be afraid, I am your friend, please come out!"

There was no reply from the saucer.

"Hey, I want to meet you, I'm not scared, you know!" (Of course, this was a lie.) There were no movements from within the spacecraft. I was getting fidgety, but somehow I managed to keep my cool and I continued to shout out, "Why don't you show yourself? You have landed here, so what do you want?"

Total silence, nobody came out from the flying-saucer.

I really started to get exasperated, but I decided to give it another try. "Hey, you inside," I pleaded. "There is no one but us around here, you have nothing to fear, so come on, please come out!"

A swishy noise began to reverberate all around the craft, interrupted at regular intervals by resounding clicks.

"What is happening now? Where is that sound coming from?" I mumbled to myself.

Swiiishshsh, tick, tick tick. Swiiishshsh, tick, tick tick. Swiiishshsh, tick, tick tick. Swiiishshsh, tick, tick tick.

The swishing sounds heightened to a formidable level, followed by incessant resounding clicks.

I covered my ears; it was now intolerable. I was confused, and hot, and all around me everything still appeared to be moving in slow motion. It was a traumatic experience. Powerful reverberations and the piercing sounds emerging from the saucer were penetrating deep inside my head. It was hurting badly and I was feeling nauseous.

For a short while I tried to resist the discomfort and intense pain that had overtaken my body. I was short of breath and felt feverish. Was I imagining all these physical discomforts? I fought hard to stay alert. Then without warning things started to move quickly around me, the buzzing of insects increased, becoming louder and louder; the smell of the lavender field became stronger; but still the noise of the flying-saucer remained clearly audible. To my great astonishment someone or something was finally stepping down the ladder.

"Oh, no, not now!" I said to myself.

From the corner of my eye. I caught a glimpse of a pair of legs standing on the steps. A bright shiny light burst out all around me. It was so white and so powerful that it blinded me and I could not see anything. A wave of heat wrapped me up and it felt as if I was lifted off the ground! I lost consciousness.

I can't say how long I remained blacked out.

CHAPTER THREE
FAMILIAR MUSIC

I regained consciousness for a moment but passed out again almost immediately. For a second, I felt that I was in a different place. When I woke up I noticed that I was in a room. The room was filled with very soft and melodious music, and a shiny brilliant light. Large spotlights on the ceiling were blinding me and I could not keep my eyes open. I was no longer nauseous; the pains in my ears and my head were gone. I was extremely thirsty and my mouth felt dry. It was then that I noticed that I was lying naked on a table. There was nobody around.

"Turn off these lights, I can't see, it's too bright! Hey, is there anybody here?

"Hey, you, I have to go, they are waiting for me at the camp!

"Hello, is there somebody here?

"Let me go! Everyone will be worried about me and they will call the police for sure!"

There was no one around and there were no answers to my pleas. I realized that I was not even restrained on the table; simply, a white sheet was covering me from the waist down.

I tried to get up, but I was still very dizzy and I fell back on the table. I closed my eyes, trying to force myself to think about this nightmare.

Where was I? Why was I naked and who had brought me here?

I could not answer any of these questions. Besides, I was exhausted and I just wanted to get back to sleep. I closed my eyes and tried to relax.

I had been snoozing for a while when I suddenly woke up to the sounds of classical music. I recognized immediately one of my favourite pieces, entitled "Bolero", by the French composer, Maurice Ravel. I was studying music at the time and I was familiar with many of the famous operas and symphonies.   As I listened, I tried to scan the room more closely. The lights had now been dimmed and it was a little easier to distinguish the various details. Right above me, I noticed an intricate system of coloured hoses and intertwined wires. There was no furniture around. It was spartan and very compact. In contrast with this simplicity, the electronic equipment seemed far ahead of the time.

I was in another world. The space was filled with what resembled TV screens. Placed on consoles or encased in wall panels was a large amount of sophisticated and scientific apparatus. The latter also supported coloured buttons, switches, curious numerical digits and levers. On my left side, a sort of movie screen was turned on but there was no image, just a bluish colour flashing on and off. A model of a celestial sphere, supported by a shiny brass holder, adorned a corner of the cabin.

The floor was made of square black-coloured tiles and the mechanical devices were mostly dark grey in colour. I may have been lying down in an operating theatre but I had no bandages nor any tubes attached to my body. In addition, I could not see any surgical equipment anywhere. – I had been lucky!

They were no doors, no exits, and no windows. The chamber was spotless, odourless and a little cool. When the "Bolero" stopped, it was replaced by Beethoven's "Fidelio". My dizziness dissipated; I sat up on the table and having done so felt fine. I decided to walk around the room and search for a way out. I used the sheet to cover myself. I thought about my family, my friends and Father Moyon at the camp. Probably they were looking for me frantically all over the region. Yes, I was in big trouble! Then I pondered why those in charge of this place played opera, and why they chose the particular pieces that I enjoyed the most? It was very strange indeed.

The chamber was extraordinary. It was, in fact, the subtle combination of a medical cubicle with the inside of the cockpit of a commercial plane. Nevertheless, the technology and scientific materials exhibited within these walls were undoubtedly unique and far too advanced for a human to comprehend. I saw strange glass tubes filled with purple, green and red liquids. But I could not decipher any of the inscriptions which appeared to have been engraved on the panels, consoles and murals. The square black floor tiles felt soft under my bare feet like the floor mat in a gymnasium.

I was looking at computers. On Earth in 1959 we did not have them yet and so they puzzled me.

"What are those?" I asked myself. "TV sets? Typewriters?" All the buttons bore signs and letters that I did not understand. I had never encountered that type of graphology before.

On the walls, I noticed some oval devices with cords hanging, which looked like flat telephones.

What intrigued me the most was the model of the celestial sphere. While examining it closely, I discerned geometrical figures which had been outlined in red, green, and black. The contours were triangles, circles, squares, ovals, and rectangles. I kept turning the globe slowly and even though the graphics, notations and configurations did not mean anything to me, I recognized the chart of the Milky Way and some of the Zodiac signs. I also found the position of our solar system, with our planet, Earth, circled in red.

What did it mean?

It seemed to confirm that the occupants of the spacecraft had planned their voyage not only in broad terms, but had carefully considered their individual landing sites as well. Now what? What was going to happen to me? It was possible that these persons from another world may have had good intentions; nevertheless at that very moment I prayed to God with all my heart, wishing that we were not flying into space with me on board. Or were we? We did not seem to be moving; at least it did not feel like it! I still had not seen or heard anyone inside the craft; I kept checking the cabin, trying to find any type of exit, but without any result. I also attempted opening what looked like cupboards and drawers, but I did not succeed. I was getting very frustrated. "Fidelio" stopped playing and almost immediately Mozart's "Figaro" began. Once again, it was music from one of my favourite compositions. As I was searching the room, I saw large bottles containing liquids of diverse colours: yellow, brown, black, and red. Each alembic was labelled with cryptic lettering. Charts and maps were engraved on heavy and slanted metallic boards. I saw a full diagram of planet Earth with green circles identifying various European countries including France.

Well, they had landed! No doubt!

One of the maps pictured Europe, Russia, and North Africa, as well as some parts of South America and the USA. On top of the maps a large sheet of hard, transparent plastic bore the marks of galactic voyages. Red dots were aligned in various positions from one end of the sheet to the other. It was obvious that these marks represented routes like "flight plans." Some dots were in single lines, others had been marked in parallel lines.

"These are our planned voyages, Gerard; they are the flight blueprints and, very accurately show some of the countries that we must visit!" a voice said. "You thought right, Gerard. Because we constantly travel across the universe, we need maps just like your sailors and aviators do. The coded colour systems differentiate the flights, the landings and/or the samplings," the voice added.

I was caught by surprise; I jumped and turned around quickly. That's when I saw him for the first time. He was very tall, at least seven feet, perhaps taller. He had shoulder-length, blond hair, a fair complexion, and was dressed in a white robe with a large belt and wore red boots. What struck me above anything else was how sparkling clean his clothes were, his white robe was almost shiny.

I did not say a word. Yes, I was scared.

"Don't be nervous, you can come closer, we need to talk. Please Gerard, you must realize that we have not hurt you in any way and that we do not intend to do so. Please relax, we are your friends, we come in peace."

His voice was calm and soothing. He spoke perfect French, without an accent.

"How do you know my name?" I asked.

"I know everything about you, you'll see," he said.

As he held out his hand, I shook it, and immediately a gush of warmth surged through my body. My anxieties, fears and disbelief were suddenly transformed into feelings of serenity and joy.

I could not comprehend it. I was not scared anymore and I felt completely relaxed. He held my hand for a few seconds longer and I looked at him more closely. His eyes met mine and I noticed how blue and piercing they were. He was not only looking at me but "through me". He had a light complexion. His lips were thick and his facial features were deeply pronounced. He smiled at me and his teeth were sparkling white. His long blond hair was curly. Under his shiny white robe he wore a white jump suit. His red boots were about knee length and spotless. His belt buckle attracted my attention and I saw that a large red stone, ruby-like, was mounted in the centre.

"You are safe, Gerard. Please get ready and we shall sit down and talk," he said.

He pointed to a wall panel, and as I approached it, he pressed a button and it slid open. In a small room I found my clothes, cleaned and wrapped in a plastic bag. The cubby hole was like a small lab with tubes, wires, TV screens, gauges, coloured buttons on wall panels, very similar to the other room. I dressed quickly and the stranger asked me to follow him. A third part of his quarters appeared to be an office and work room combined. We both sat down at a table on two very comfortable chairs. There was a TV set in the centre of the table.

"Are you hungry or thirsty, Gerard?" he asked.

"Thirsty, thank you."

The stranger walked to a wall panel, pressed a button and returned with a metallic cup of blue liquid.

"It is healthy and tasty, Gerard. It contains what you call on your planet vitamins," he said.

I did, in fact, find the drink fresh and delicious.

"How long have I been here?" I questioned.

"Not very long," he replied.

"How do you know my name?" I asked again.

"We have a lot of information about you and all the other persons that we visit on Earth. I will soon show you."

CHAPTER FOUR
EUDOXUS

Gerard, let me explain to you why we came here, and what happened while you were asleep. My detailed clarifications will surely answer many of your questions. However, Gerard, I must be brief this time, as I must leave soon.

"My name is Eudoxus; I come from the planet Toki very far away in the galaxy. Our spacecraft is manned by several people who have their specialties. You will not meet them. While you were sleeping, we did some tests on you but you will not suffer any effects from them. You have absolutely no marks on your body. The tests gave us information, that's all. We noticed that you have had two serious surgeries since birth but you are in perfect health now. You have a very strong constitution. You do remember, as I mentioned earlier, that we often fly over countries, sometimes we just land and observe and occasionally we take specimens. They can be in the form of plants, vegetables, soil, animals and even human beings. This time it was "you". You should know, Gerard, that you were not selected at random. Toki has sent our people to Earth many times before. It is my fourth voyage to your region of France. I came here in 1952, 1953, 1956 and again now. We follow strict and pre-arranged patterns for our flights. We come back to certain countries over and over again. We also fly over oceans, mountains and continents as many times as we find it necessary for our studies. We analyse all sorts of life forms such as insects, reptiles, fishes, and mammals – including humans. You were selected because of your distinctive qualities. You are quite unique in fighting adversity. It's an innate gift. We search for people such as yourself who possess various qualities, talents, genius perhaps and we meet them personally, like I am doing right now with you. On some occasions we have taken such a human specimen on board for a voyage, but it will not happen today, so do not be nervous."

Eudoxus stopped talking and looked at me. I was tense but extremely interested in his story. I started to ask a question but he interrupted me.

"You are a fighter and a survivor, these are very rare abilities," he said. "Please look at the screen and you will notice that I have all the necessary information about you."

He entered data on the keyboard and my picture came up with my personal data shown underneath. It showed my medical history, my school marks, my hobbies, and the sports that I practiced. It was amazing. Next to my name, the word "specimen" was written in red. It was exactly like Eudoxus had said.

"I have never seen such a piece of equipment before, even at the movies. What is it?" I asked.

"It is called a computer and it registers information, but in addition, it processes data and gives us all the results of our work very rapidly. It is extremely complex. It will be widely used on Earth in the coming decades. It is, however, ahead of your time at the present.

"I cannot explain to you all the reasons at this time. You cannot understand yet the scientific and technical facts of our expeditions. Therefore, I will only say that our tests, experiments and the specimens that we physically remove from planet Earth are essential to us and the inhabitants of your world. You will realize over the years that what we are doing has great purpose. You will clearly understand the truth. All in all, in order to improve your living conditions and ours, we must keep doing research work incessantly. That is one of my functions on Toki. I am what you call on Earth an astronomer, a philosopher and a mathematician.

"I do not like math," I said to him.

"Yes, I know, I can see your marks; but you are an artist and you are a very good student in languages," he laughed.

"How big is this spacecraft?" I asked.

"Unfortunately, we won't tour it, but it is rather small for us. You saw it from the outside. We have other spaceships, some are larger, a few are small, but we mainly take off and land from our mother ships. They are very, very large, huge.

"Tell me, Eudoxus, have you taken other people to your planet, or even animals?" I asked.

"Rarely, but I investigate many countries on Earth and also travel to other galaxies. I can tell you that I have spoken and seen many people from various backgrounds, such as singers, actors, policemen, fire-fighters, soldiers, pilots, sailors and more. You are in fact one of the few children that I have met. Again, you are in very good health and you are also a very special person. Please understand and remember that. I also know from your record that you have faith and that you are very religious. It is very important and honourable to be the way you are and please do not change. Stay the same."

"What do you mean, Eudoxus? I am nothing very special. In fact I wish that I were a better student or even better at sports than I am!" I replied.

"No, Gerard, you are a good boy. You are smart and you have a good heart. Stay happy, enjoy life! You are very mature for a twelve-year-old and that is why I am talking to you right now. I do not predict the future. I am not a fortune-teller. I am real, but we have capacities that are far ahead of yours. Believe what I say. You are going to go through a very challenging life which will be like a roller-coaster. At times, it will be all dark around you, but you will overcome your difficulties victoriously. Your faith and your beliefs will help you to succeed. Spiritually Gerard, you are a child of the light! You have a lot to say to people, you are a great communicator. Your entire existence may perhaps be spent in helping others. You are lucky! Be happy and proud. I feel that sometimes you are misunderstood and not necessarily appreciated for what you really are. But you can overcome anything that is thrown at you! Gerard, a lot of people will envy you!"

"Have you been visiting planets for long?" I asked.

"For decades, Gerard. There are many planets and galaxies in the universe. We simply try to understand how other people live, and if possible, improve each other's conditions. Some of our people already coexist among you."

"What do you mean?" I asked Eudoxus.

"Well, they look like you, dress, eat, and talk like you. They set up a base on Earth and after a certain period, once they have gathered enough information, we come back and pick them up. It's simply scientific research. I know that it sounds very bizarre to you, but we have been here for a very long time. We know what is happening on Earth. But this is very good proof that we are not the enemy. We are peaceful people. Toki is a very nice planet."

"Will you tell me, Eudoxus, what life is like on Toki?"

"I cannot this time, Gerard. I have not much time left. But one day, I will come back. I will always know where you are and then we shall talk longer."

"I wish that I could have my picture taken with you," I said.

"Not possible, and it would not work anyway. No picture, no recording, nothing would work. I came only to meet you. To reassure you that what you saw was just an experiment. You are in no danger."

"But, Eudoxus, I have a lot of questions to ask you. You have explained a few things to me, but I would like to know more. For example, do all people from space look like you?" I asked him.

"No, but we on our planet closely resemble the people of Earth. Many other planets have other types of alien, who do not look like you at all. That is why we can visit Earth easily and stay among you for long periods. We are tall, but otherwise we are not particularly noticeable. We also dress like you and that makes it much easier to move around freely. Again, some other planets have very different types of living forms. But I cannot tell you about it now."

"Eudoxus, what about my friends who have witnessed the landing? What is going to happen to me at the camp when I return and what shall I tell Father Moyon and the police, or my family who must all be looking for me frantically at the moment?" I was very concerned and almost crying.

Eudoxus simply smiled at me. Once again he looked at me with his deep blue eyes and a strange feeling descended upon me. I calmed down immediately.

He said to me: "Gerard, nothing bad or punitive is going to take place. I want to assure you that nobody has witnessed the landing. That is why you did not hear any motorists honk or stop to investigate, and you didn't observe any boats cruising on the river. No one can see us even as we speak. Your friends, Jose and Richard, have already returned to camp after they stopped at the farm to collect milk, eggs, and fresh tomatoes as Father Moyon requested. They were both treated to a nice lunch by the local farmers. They do not remember anything about the landing. It has been obliterated from their memories. When Father Moyon inquired about your absence and your whereabouts, he was told by Jose and Richard that you had stayed behind at the farm to witness the birth of a new foal. A mare gave birth to a foal approximately one hour ago. They will call it Texas, like in America."

I was totally flabbergasted, but I managed a few words. "Eudoxus," I stammered. "How can this be possible? How do you know about the foal and its name? Frankly speaking, a few hours must have passed since the landing. Everyone must be looking for me! How can this spacecraft suddenly become invisible? My friends and I watched this big black machine come down with a lot of noise, lights and a lot of coloured smoke all around it. It is incredible!" I retorted.

"Gerard, they are expecting you to return late to the camp because of Texas's birth. Do not worry." He then added, "Gerard, I cannot give you all the reasons behind my answers nor can I explain the scientific intricacies, but please believe me when I say that no one, absolutely no one has seen us or is even seeing us right now as we speak. Once you reach the camp, you will realize that you are not a missing person.

"Nobody can see us because there is a very advanced defense system built within the craft that we can use whenever it is necessary. It makes us invisible.

"The fact that you have not been missing for too long from the camp is a complex phenomenon, called a time warp. You would not understand it."

But suddenly I interrupted him. "Eudoxus, Jose and Richard were with me in the field, they saw it all! By now they must have told everyone about the spacecraft."

"No, Gerard, I repeat that they will not remember anything apart from their task to fetch Father Moyon's food order, which they completed. You are the only person who will remember our meeting and conversations, only you Gerard."

I was feeling very uneasy when listening to this statement.

"But Eudoxus, what did you do to them?" I asked.

"Nothing that hurt them, Gerard," he answered. "When we land the spacecraft, a large screen, invisible to human eyes, covers a large perimeter around the entire ship. It has a security purpose; however, the main function of this system is to cleanse any foreign body coming in and out of the craft. It also washes all memories of the experience. For Jose and Richard, the incident never took place. There was no harm done," he explained.

"Eudoxus, how many languages do you speak?" I asked.

"Whenever I go, I learn the language. For us, it is only a matter of assimilating a particular magnetic tape. It does not take me more than an hour to learn a foreign tongue fluently. I have to tell you that other planets have many diverse dialects as well."

Eudoxus at that point looked at me again and stood up. He left the room and went to another part of the spacecraft through sliding panels. I did not know what to think, it was an unbelievable experience and the most interesting part was that I was no longer scared of the situation.

However, I was still wary in regard to what Eudoxus had said.

Jose and Richard would not remember the landing?

The time warp factor?

The certitude that I would not be too late getting back to camp?

The invisible flying-saucer? – No one would have noticed a flying object measuring about 95 metres in circumference in the middle of a field?

All this was too much to swallow all at once.

Eudoxus came back and said to me, "I will have to leave very soon; the engineer has almost finished his work."

"What type of activity is he performing?" I asked.

"We take many specimens of natural elements from your planet. It helps us compare activities, life forms, reproduction, habitats; and it measures the life expectancy of creatures and/or even of planets. It is purely scientific research."

"Eudoxus, I have so many questions to ask you, but you say you must go away! Are you going to come back?" I inquired.

"I will, Gerard. But I do not know where and when I will visit Earth and the South of France next. Some areas of your planet are extremely interesting for our experiments and we fly over certain specific countries because they provide magnetic energy to our spacecraft."

"How so, Eudoxus?"

"You call them vortices on your planet, and they spread over certain parts of Earth, very often in straight lines. You could say that we recharge our batteries, as an automobile does, simply by flying over those parts of Earth at lower altitude. That is when your people can see us and often get very scared. But as you realize, we do not mean any harm; on the contrary, we come in peace to collect information."

I inquired, "What are the areas which are considered vortices?"

And he replied: "To name a few: South America, France, Belgium, England, Morocco, India, Switzerland, Canada, the USA, Russia, the Caribbean Islands, the Himalayas and more. They are conduits of radioactivity which provides generated power and an essential flow of energy for our fleet."

I asked him another question. "Eudoxus what is going to happen to me now? After you leave, what should I do? What should I say? If you did not want me to remember anything at all, why did you speak to me and explain all these details to me?"

"Gerard, contrary to what you may think, I want you to remember everything which has taken place; however, I have only discussed a few basic points of astronomy with you, since I would never divulge any special flight plans or sensitive matters pertaining to our missions. You would be too young to understand their intricate technicalities anyway. But again, you will recall the landing with all the details that followed, without suffering any side effects, memory loss, disturbing nightmares and above all, without any inner torments. As a matter of fact, you will soon begin to sense some soothing, peaceful and spiritual sensations within you. You are going to receive a surge of energy.

"Gerard, you now have solid proof that UFOs do exist. In addition, you have learned that the universe consists of galaxies, millions of planets bearing other intelligent life forms, and that Earth is only a small part of the cosmos. You have witnessed what only a select few have the chance to observe. Remember, there is a reason why you were selected out of all others.

"Be patient, you know the truth; therefore, please don't mind those people who are incredulous. You will have your place in this world and it is not going to be because of luck, since you will work very hard for what you will later earn and possess. Gerard, you have been blessed with an innate supply of energy. You are not a quitter! I want to add that you will be admired by many."

"Eudoxus, people are very scared of flying-saucers and aliens! We are always at war with citizens from other planets in the movies! Newspapers claim that whoever sees a UFO is crazy; Eudoxus do you understand why I cannot disclose our meeting? No one will ever believe me, even my parents will call me a liar!"

"Gerard, I understand your worries and that is why I promise you that you are the only one person today who has witnessed this landing. We have talked together, but what has been said is only between you and me. You will not talk about this encounter to anyone until you are ready to do so. When the time is right and only then, without any pressure placed upon you, you will reveal this extraordinary adventure. Not before. I want to tell you something else, which eventually you will notice as you grow older. The various governments of planet Earth are ignorant, scared and obtuse in regard to space research and astronomy overall. Few countries understand the importance and unlimited possibilities which are accessible across the galaxies. It will slowly improve over the next decades, but only two or three major countries will lead the way. Space is the way of the future because Earth will become over-populated and will run out of all essential energies. I am speaking the truth and you Gerard might even witness what I am saying within your lifetime."

I was baffled by his words and his frankness.

"Eudoxus, do all people on Toki have the same powers as you?"

"Power is the wrong word to use, Gerard. It can be dangerous and harmful if placed in the wrong hands. You will eventually realize what I am saying.

"To answer your question, on Toki we do not have powers. We nurture education, knowledge, special qualities and even special strengths. We have been taught how to control our minds, spirits, physical abilities and all the gifts which were given and passed unto us. We are a blessed planet. On Toki we do not have famine, wars, greed, epidemics; we are not over-populated, in fact it is a very well controlled environment. However, I can tell you that throughout the universe many other planets are in trouble and on the way to extinction. Your planet, Gerard, is presently in very good condition, but humans can destroy anything very quickly. That is why we travel through space to watch, help, and, if necessary, warn citizens when the situation gets too chaotic. Every single day, planets and/or stars disappear from the cosmos due to their citizens' own faults. It is horrible to watch."

"Eudoxus, will you ever contact me again?" I asked. "There is so much that I want to talk to you about!"

"You probably will not see me again in person, but I will contact you somehow in different ways such as sending you a spiritual message from time to time or an energy boost if you need it badly, and even a morale uplift when you are morose. I do the same with some of the people that I have visited and this is my way to show them that they are special. In any case, Gerard, please keep reading and studying. I want to let you know that as of today your interest in astronomy and UFOs will increase. You know that we exist and that there is life on other planets."

"Please, Eudoxus, tell me if people on Toki believe in God!"

"Gerard, this is a very deep subject and religion is very personal to each particular individual; however, to answer your question in general terms, I will ask you a question in answer to yours, if I may. Do you think that this entire planet where you presently live and all the galaxies in the infinite universe just happen to be there because of luck, for instance?"

"No, of course not!" I answered.

"You're right, Gerard! This beautiful universe had to be created for a reason, it was formed and it changes, and improvements still occur. Discoveries will be made as decades and centuries go by.

"To answer your question though, yes, people on Toki do believe in a supreme being."

Eudoxus left his seat and once again went through the sliding doors to another room. He came back and told me that all necessary specimens and data had been collected.

He was going to leave. I felt sad and I wanted him to answer many more questions.

"Gerard, one of the reasons that you were selected, if I may say so, is that, in July 1947, in the USA, a spacecraft crashed in New Mexico in a place called Roswell. You do not know anything about it, but it was very important news on Earth at that time. We were informed on Toki of that disaster. The date of that incident coincides with your birth date and because you also lived through miraculous surgery – the first attempt at a pyloric stenosis in France – I wanted to meet you. You have the strongest heart that a human can have. You were operated (at birth) on your stomach without anesthesia. We looked at   it   while   you were asleep. Were you aware of this information?"

"My parents told me about the surgery at birth, but that's all," I answered.

Then I started on a different topic. "Eudoxus, there is one thing bothering me about what you said earlier."

"What is it, Gerard?"

"I cannot lie to Father Moyon; it's impossible, Eudoxus."

"Why would you have to, in the first place?"

"You told me, Eudoxus that, one hour or more ago, a foal was born at the farm and that the reason given to Father Moyon for my tardiness is that I stayed behind to watch the birthing. I did not. I was with you the whole time. I could not be in two places at the same time. As a matter of principle, I do not lie. I cannot, Eudoxus, something is very wrong."

"You are perfectly correct, Gerard, but as I have mentioned to you before, the time warp will take care of that difference. Your time is different from ours. We operate and live on a separate speed mode. You'll see for yourself at the farm. I must again congratulate you, for you are a person with strong principles; you have integrity, honesty and values in life. You are only twelve years old but these precious and beautiful qualities will stay with you for ever. People will respect you for them. They are part of the reason that you were selected by us."

"Eudoxus, I am very intrigued by the large stone that you wear on your belt buckle; what is it?" I asked.

"It's called Mathesus. It has medicinal, healing and energizing faculties. This stone has a natural stimulant agent inside but this mineral can only be found on Toki. We use it only in extreme emergencies and whenever we do, only certain leaders and a selected group of scientists can activate its powers. I can say that the citizens of Toki own their high levels of physical fitness and motivation to Mathesus. We control its usage but we still apply it when needed."

"How old are you, Eudoxus?"

"Age is irrelevant on Toki, Gerard. It does not exist and we do not get old as on Earth. We travel from planet to planet, across the universe and the cosmos. For instance, a single flight in our spacecraft may represent thousands of years in relation to your time. So let's say that I am ageless!"

"Eudoxus, how do you find Mathesus stone on Toki?"

"We search for minerals on Toki just as we search for minerals on Earth. We extract it from rocks, caves, mountains or mines, but also from the bottoms of rivers, lakes and oceans. Mathesus stone should not be confused with the precious ruby which it resembles. Like rubies, its reddish colour makes it easy to detect. It has more value and benefits to us than mere monetary worth."

Eudoxus left the table again. He went to the next cabin. After a few minutes, he came back to announce that the crew had completed the necessary tests and that it was time to leave.

"Gerard, I must say that it was very interesting to meet you. I made the right choice by selecting you as a specimen. I will be contacting you in the future and you will always know when the time comes. Please be assured that some of the questions you were not able to ask me today will be answered at some point of time in the future. What you may perceive as secrets and mysteries, or even the unknown, will be revealed with clarity when you need the information the most. Please, Gerard, remember the message that I am giving you now!" He continued with great emphasis. "Nothing will be coincidental throughout your life, because you have been selected to witness the truth; somehow, you will find ways to tell the world your story. You have exceptional talents, particularly on the artistic side. You must use them! Trust me when I say that the day you decide to tell your story, you will not pass for a lunatic. People will respect you and believe you!"

"Eudoxus, if you are leaving, what do you want me to do now?"

"Gerard, we are a little late in our take-off proceedings, but we shall catch up on the time lost without any difficulties. The engineers are presently modifying the operating modes to depart from Earth. It will take only a few minutes for the craft to reach the cosmos. We can attain acceleration speeds which are immeasurably faster than any of your most powerful fighter planes."

"Eudoxus, may I touch the Mathesus stone before you leave?"

"As a matter of fact, Gerard, I was going to ask you to do so as part of our parting process. Please take the stone and hold it with both hands! Now close your eyes and clear your mind!" Eudoxus said, while handing me the gem.

I followed his directions and the reddish stone began to glow intensely. I felt a warm and tingling sensation inside my body. A very bright light flashed in my face. I tried to call Eudoxus, but no words came from my mouth. All of a sudden I had become dumb.

"It's happening again!" I thought. "But what is it that is happening?" I wondered to myself.

The light became brighter as I sensed its warm beams upon my face. I was not scared, but was happy, totally relaxed and wrapped in extreme jubilance.

The Mathesus stone was now pulsating within the palms of my hands and I began to weep uncontrollably. Even though I still could not communicate, I was laughing and crying at the same time. I was holding the Mathesus stone with all my might and it was injecting inner strength into my entire system. The consciousness of this was thrilling. A buzzing noise emerged from inside the spaceship. It grew louder and louder as the seconds went by and the light became brighter and brighter, reaching incandescence. Suddenly I felt my body rise slowly off the floor and I realized that I was floating in the cabin in a vertical position.

CHAPTER FIVE
KEEPING A SECRET

From a vertical position, I started to oscillate and amidst rays of blinding light I moved horizontally. I was feeling comfortable, did not suffer any pain, and I was still alert and aware of what was going on around me. I was clutching the stone in my hands and there was a warm tingling throughout my body. I was levitating.

I heard Eudoxus' voice saying, "Good-bye Gerard, it's time to part. Relax now and as soon as you wake up, go to the farm nearby. Everything is going to be fine."

At that moment, I began to experience flashbacks, pictures moving fast before my eyes: Jose and Richard watching the landing, butterflies flying above the lavender field, the spacecraft hovering and making a strident noise, the room with its strange TV sets and coloured pipes, Eudoxus standing in front of me wearing his red boots, the stone with its bright red reflections. All of these images were very real and they were penetrating my brain. My eyes were still open and I screamed and screamed again, squeezing the Mathesus stone with all my might.

Without warning, I found myself enveloped in a complete sensory black-out. There was total darkness around me; there were no smells, no sounds, nothing was moving: but I was still floating horizontally. I lost consciousness.

I opened my eyes, I felt something wet on my face.

Slurp, slurp, slurp! Two big dark eyes were looking at me. I jumped up yelling and the dog which was licking my cheek and nose ran away barking.

The sun was high in the blue sky and the bees, flies, and butterflies were all buzzing and dancing above the lavender field.

I could distinguish a golden corn-patch and heard the river flowing close by, I was relieved that this entire episode had come to an end.

A couple of trucks and automobiles drove past me and instinctively I waved at them, they honked and I knew then that I was not dreaming.

It was very, very hot and I walked toward the river to cool off and clear my head.

I dipped my head into the water and felt much better. I sat down trying to piece together, in a rational manner, the last moments of my unique adventure. I was floating inside the craft amidst flashing bright lights, not scared, and Eudoxus was giving me his last instructions. That's all I could remember; this UFO landing had never taken place!

Because I wanted to be sure that no traces had been left around the landing site, I carefully paced the entire perimeter one more time scrutinizing everything for the smallest clue. I could not find anything at all, it was unbelievable!

Eudoxus had not left me any substantial proof. Hence I was on my own and I had to prepare myself accordingly. "The secret" was to remain with me for ever. I decided to walk toward the farm and hopefully be on time to witness the birth of the new foal named Texas! At that moment I was totally confused and somehow curious about what I was going to find out at the grange. I did not know what time it was and I was rushing as fast as I could.

I had difficulty concentrating while walking and certain words and sentences kept coming back into my head: *time-warp, specimen, computers, innate energy, Toki, Mathesus stone, child of the light, experiment*, so many new terms to absorb and comprehend!

Even so, I was starting to notice the colourful countryside and the smell of Provence again. I stopped for a few minutes to look at the river and watch a couple of young people fishing. I suddenly realized that I was lucky to be home rather than on a flying-saucer travelling across the galaxy. Yes, I was a lucky boy indeed. I turned around and looked at the corn field and the lavender patch on the edge of the water.

"Yes, it did happen for sure," I said to myself aloud.

Soon I saw houses on the horizon.

As I was approaching the farm, wheels were spinning inside my head. "It will be very hard to keep this encounter from my family, Father Moyon and my two friends Jose and Richard," I thought, "particularly, when it is meant to be an everlasting secret."

I turned around, and looked up at the sky. For a brief second, I saw Eudoxus. Then I glanced at the golden and purple patches of corn and lavender, and asked myself: How did they do it?

How could such a large flying object, probably weighing several tons, and resting on four heavy metallic legs thrust into soft ground, disappear without a trace? How could it possibly happen? It defied all logic. I had not found any burn marks, foreign objects, or prints in the entire area.

The trees, bushes, leaves, and flowers – including the corn and lavender stalks – had all been left apparently untouched by the UFO. If there was any soil blown over and scattered around the edges of the fields, well, the wind could have done it.

Eudoxus had said that in 1952, 1953, and 1956, we in Provence had been visited by them; and now I remembered my father telling me about it.

CHAPTER SIX
THE BLACK CIRCLE

As I walked to the farm, I thought over a few of the amazing anecdotes about UFOs that had made the international news. One was about "the black circle". Around 1952 and 1953 flying-saucer sightings in the south of France had increased.

On one particular occasion, a large spaceship hovered above an agricultural area outside Aix-en-Provence at approximately 2pm the gendarmes were called and also witnessed the incident. For a period of fifteen minutes the saucer hung in the air, at about three metres above ground, on the same spot. When it took off, the entire area was illuminated by such a bright light that nobody saw the UFO leave the field. There was no explosion, very little smell, no fumes. People just remembered an extraordinary brightness covering the entire district. The acceleration was phenomenal and later the military authorities stated that no plane, from anywhere around the world, could fly at such speed in 1953. There were however a few traces and indelible marks left by the "visitors". Trees, gates, and shacks located close to the landing site had been burned to ashes. The main buildings were not damaged and there were no victims. The pictures of the hovering UFO taken and later processed by the gendarmes had come out blank.

It was understood that when the UFO departed, the power created by the acceleration was so intense that it produced the blinding light people saw and its reactors had burned everything in sight. That is obviously a very simple explanation, but that is all we could deduce from this experience in 1953. People had realized that, perhaps, the "visitors" were not necessarily ill-meaning; after all they had stayed just a short time and did not kill anybody.

All the road signs and the asphalt adjacent to the property had melted. A small artificial lake behind the tree line close to the farm was empty and dry. Vehicles which had stopped to watch the UFO – including police cars – could not start again for at least one hour and their tyres melted. And last but not least, the spacecraft imprinted its shape on the field; it left a perfect black circle in the soil. Yet the crop around the mark remained intact.

The story goes that, for years afterwards, the farmer kept cultivating the land as usual, but nothing, absolutely nothing, grew ever again in that circular patch. The soil both within and outside the circle was analysed, and a very high level of radioactivity was found. As a result, the owner could not sell any of his farm products commercially anymore. However, he still kept growing fresh products for his own consumption. But the "circle" remained bare. He just could not produce anything from that particular patch of land. Nothing grew on it. The farmer achieved some notoriety and received a wide range of press coverage. Consequently, people from all over the world came to see the mysterious "black circle".

In 1956, the South of France was hit by a very unusual cold winter. Snow, ice-storms, and blizzards paralyzed the Riviera and Provence. The entire region was engulfed in at least one metre of white powdery snow. It was a nightmare! There was no equipment to clear the roads. And once again the farm made the news! The whole field was covered with a thick white coat with the exception of a perfect black circle where the snowflakes immediately melted upon touching the ground. Photographs of this scene made front page news around the world. This is a true story! My father drove me to the area years later and I saw the imprint in the ground with my own eyes.

Remembering this authentic event was quite timely considering the circumstances that had just transpired, as well as the fact that UFOs had always intrigued me personally.

Another extraordinary case came to my mind: "the black-out of 1957." It was a centre of attraction in the South of France as well as a focus in UFO history.

One summer night in 1957, a large fleet of flying-saucers flew over our region. Newspaper and radio broadcasts mentioned that the number reached six hundred but that was only an estimate. This time pictures were taken at high altitude by the French Air Force. Long rows of white circles (the UFOs) were quite apparent in the black sky. The pictures made worldwide news and the media used them abundantly. Unlike the landing of 1956 when the pictures taken and processed by the French gendarmes had come out blank, the French Air Force managed to take numerous shots of the spacecraft and the photos were very clear. The air chase lasted more than thirty minutes and the comments made by French "Top Guns" were quite amazing! They had never taken part in or even witnessed a mission on such a scale.

The pilots described the spacecraft as large, circular, shiny objects. They could see no trace of living forms inside since there were no windows nor portholes on the machines.

The fleet was moving at incredible speed, but no sign of combustion to operate the craft could be discerned; obviously their mode of propulsion came entirely from within. When the French pilots managed to get close to the saucers, they noticed that their shiny appearance had been transformed into a dull, dark, metallic colour. Was it some type of protection? Or perhaps it was a system established to appear less conspicuous?

Suddenly this large group of foreign objects moved at full speed and disappeared into space without a trace!

The French "Top Guns" were flabbergasted and claimed that no jet fighter-plane on Earth at that time (1957) could have flown away at such speed. One second they were all lined up in the sky, flying in a perfect military formation, the next they had vanished in a bright flashing light without making a sound. Right in front of their eyes!

Imagine six hundred unidentified flying objects vanishing all at once, in a flash, while being pursued by the French Air Force!

The pursuit lasted approximately thirty minutes but absolutely no information had been gathered by the military. It seemed six hundred spacecraft had flown away undetected. No radio contact, no speed levels, no points of entry or exit: but photographs had been taken and they made the front pages worldwide.

There was more to the story.

While flying over France, this large group of UFOs had drawn a tremendous amount of energy from the ground. Because it was night time, most of the inhabitants were home and thus witnessed the "black-out" incident. It was as if a supernatural force pulled all electrical power to the sky! Every single engine, turbine, battery, and dynamo went dead. As the spacecraft hovered over various parts of the country, all lights and telecommunications stopped. The town of Aix-en-Provence remained in pitch darkness for more than an hour.

It was pure chaos everywhere. Emergency supplies could not be restored and patients were left helpless on hospital operating tables. People were trapped in elevators. Highway road lights and traffic lights did not work. Very precarious situations arose when facilities such as police stations, dams, airports, hospitals, train and bus stations, water purification plants and other common facilities ceased to function.

The newspapers called this event: "A Hell of a Night!" The South of France was a subject of sensationalism and at the same time a new passage for UFOs travelling Earth! The media fed on these occurrences for a long time and they loved it!

Similar circumstances surrounding the 1957 "black-out" in the South of France occurred in North America in 1962. It was very well documented with a lot of pictures to support it.

Government officials in the USA and Canada blamed power failures at Niagara Falls and Buffalo on the incident. Hundreds of pictures were taken but the public at large was still baffled by the mysterious UFOs. In addition, the military, the air force and the national security agencies involved would not confirm the story. Instead, they persisted in maintaining that power failures were responsible for the chaos. In those days, the topic of flying-saucers and "little green men" was very sensitive; for those involved in investigating such phenomena, keeping information secret was a way to make the news disappear more quickly.

Soon, however, it became impossible to ignore the UFO phenomenon any longer. Consistent with this, Canada built classified centres at strategic locations across the country, with very specific objectives: to observe, assemble, and analyse as much evidence as possible and report any UFO activities to the government. A thousand plus flying-saucers crossing the Canadian night sky are not very easy to hide, and on that night in 1962 all of these centres accumulated masses of information to record and analyse. However, a little while later all the centres were shut down without notice. Why did the Canadian government act in this way? Why build those extremely expensive centres for nothing? What did they find out on that night? And why were the scientists involved sworn to secrecy? No one ever knew.

In the years that followed, a few high-profile sightings and landings occurred over and in the Canadian provinces. Following the 1962 passage of spaceships across North American skies, Canada became famous as part of the UFO scene. As the encounters increased, scientists from all over the world came to analyse the sites.

One of the most controversial episodes occurred in Nova Scotia when a large flying object crashed into a small town harbour during the night. The ocean was not very deep at the point of impact and the spacecraft's lights were still glowing under the water when the navy divers who were called in to investigate the site arrived on the scene. Immediately, everyone who participated in the search was sworn to total secrecy; they were told that this event had not even taken place. Some frogmen refused to return to work after their first dive, genuinely scared by something out of the ordinary. Within a few hours the navy stopped the underwater search because more divers were reluctant to approach the foreign object.

The details that emerged from that night were rather sketchy. Locals did confirm that a very eerie and unusual atmosphere descended upon the village that particular evening.

Canadian investigators confirmed two points: first, that US scientists had been invited to participate in the final enquiry; and second, that the UFO had been transported to an air-force base in the Nevada desert. Was it site 51? No one knew for sure. One fact was certain, the flying-saucer had mysteriously disappeared from the harbour and the whole affair was put to rest. The Canadian government denied the reports as usual. Over the years, movies, books, and TV series have tried to corroborate the crash but the mystery has never been explained.

All round the world, in the 1950s and 1960s, many high ranking government officials, including the military top brass and prominent scientists, were discredited and even fired from their jobs when they maintained the existence of flying-saucers and testified that aliens from other planets had landed on Earth.

Proofs of UFO sightings and close encounters have been substantiated for centuries by way of carvings, sketches and frescos of all sorts that have been found in pyramids, caves and religious temples all around the world. Large statues, sculptures, murals and totems have depicted, "Foreign gods coming from above and landing on Earth." Under hypnosis, people who had been snatched by aliens remembered going through medical examinations aboard the spacecraft. In most cases, they claimed that the experiments made on them had been painful and traumatic.

Once returned safely to Earth, the kidnap victims suffered from amnesia.

Microscopic implants were found inside their vital organs. What were the reasons for these surgeries? Were they placed inside their bodies to be used as tracking devices?

All in all space kidnappings remain an enigma to this day.

I had at some time managed to read a few clippings about the famous incident which took place in July 1947 in Roswell, New Mexico.

The US Air Force has always vehemently denied the incident. The result has been twofold. First, the story has been completely twisted and later it came to be ignored.

It was to become the largest cover-up ever in UFO history. Flying-saucers, bodies of aliens and secret equipment, which had been found aboard the spacecraft, were acquired by the US Air Force and hidden secretly in the Nevada desert. Was it true or not? No one knows for sure. But in 1964, the US Air Force produced a final statement explaining to the public at large that weather balloons were the cause of this unfortunate controversy. Throughout the inquiries, major witnesses were challenged, discredited and – even more – their lives were threatened. Ever since then, TV shows, books, and major motion pictures have been depicting the incident.

Nevertheless, there has never been any concrete proof to the effect that a flying-saucer and its occupants crashed in Roswell, and that following the crash, all the evidence was transported to a secret place in the Nevada desert.

CHAPTER SEVEN
TEXAS

I had now reached the farm. The distinctive smells of the homestead including the smell of manure were stronger than normal. Chickens, pigs, hens, cats, and dogs were all running loose; a rooster was strutting proudly on a heap of hay. Behind the corner of the main house stood a large field where horses, ponies and cows were grazing peacefully.

On the other side of the patch, a little grey donkey was feeding calmly on the fresh grass.

I walked curiously around the perimeter among ducks, pigeons and large black flies.

I noticed a brick stone well with empty buckets resting on its edge.

The farm was a beautiful, large and rustic property. A tall silo painted red bore a sign on its roof reading: "Private Property, No Visitors Please!"

Walking behind a large barn, I passed by some wire cages holding geese, black and white rabbits, and pheasants; and in a restricted area I saw two wild boar lying in a pool of mud.

Under the blue sky and the hot sun, and amid this marvelous scenery, the farmhouse looked very animated and picturesque.

I found the kitchen door at the back of the central wing of the house.

I stepped inside and the farmer's wife came to meet me. She was cooking and the smell was wonderful. She seemed to be in a hurry.

"Hello, what can I do for you, young man?" she asked.

"My name is Gerard and I am with Father Moyon's camp. I believe that two of my friends came earlier to pick up the food that had been ordered. I was supposed to stay with them, but I somehow got lost. I know I am late but is there anything for me to fetch? If so, I'll take it to the camp."

"There is one last bag left and it's all ready for you. But before you take it and leave, would you like to come with me to the stable? I have to rush back there, as a mare is about to give birth to a new foal. I'm sure you have never witnessed such an event. It will be the most productive science lesson that you've ever had. It will be more real than books or a classroom lecture. Do you think that you can handle it?" she asked.

"Sure, I would love to watch," I answered.

"In that case, please follow me," she said.

In the stable, a large mare was lying on hay and she seemed as if she was about to die. She was in terrible distress. Her eyes were wide open and her pupils and nostrils were dilated. Her whole body was sweating profusely. She was making strange puffing noises, and because she was suffering, her neighs were strident. Her mouth was wide open showing large grinding teeth.

I had to turn my head a few times because there was a lot of blood and frankly speaking witnessing the birth of the foal was quite an ordeal. It was all new to me and I could say that it was a new life lesson as far as I was concerned. I never forgot it. The farmers were remarkable in the way that they handled the mare's suffering. Finally after just under two hours of labour a beautiful new foal was born. A very apologetic veterinarian arrived late since he had been detained 40 kilometres away at another location. He double checked, the mare, the foal, and the barn and he asked the farmers some questions.

He wrote down some directives and prescriptions to follow and explained that he would be back within the next 48 hours to make sure that there was no trace of infection. Both the mare and the foal appeared in perfect health.

I still remember this extraordinary experience to this day.

The farmers had really impressed me by the way they had planned and helped the new foal's arrival. Everyone had kept their cool. They had gathered together the necessary supplies for the delivery. Two helpers and the farmers' children had talked softly to the mare, constantly massaging her big belly in order to ease the strain, acting as nurses all the way through the event. They fetched water, blankets, towels and whatever they were asked to fetch throughout the time. It was obvious that they had performed these tasks many times before. They kept their confidence and sense of humour through it all.

I admired them not only for their expertise but also for the love and care they gave the animals at the farm; they were true professionals.

Once the foal was born, the mare rested calmly and everyone seemed very cheerful.

The owner's daughter suddenly announced with a great big smile: "I have a name for the new foal!"

"What are you going to call him?" her father asked.

"Texas!" she said, "like the state in America!"

"It sounds like a real western name," answered her brother. "It's too American."

"Sure, and I think that it is quite appropriate," replied the daughter. "Without horses, there would not be any westerns."

"Let your sister decide; you picked the name when the last foal was born. It's your sister's turn now," said the mother. And that was the end of it.

The foal was now sleeping beside his mother and the colour of his coat was a reddish light brown, almost rusty. It would darken as the weeks went by. There was no doubt that Texas was going to grow up to be a very healthy and strong horse.

I walked out of the barn, still in shock. Wow! I had just witnessed the birth of a foal. Earlier I had seen the landing of a UFO, and on top of that I had met an alien in his spacecraft. All in one day!

Anyone would think that I was a lucky guy, but I was not so sure anymore.

"Hey Gerard, how did you find the birthing?" asked the mother of the family at the farm.

"Fine, really," I answered.

"You look a little white, Boy. Are you okay?" she asked.

"Yes, yes, no problems. I just need to relax for a few minutes, that's all. I'm going to walk back to the camp; I'll be fine by the time I reach the site. Thank you again for the opportunity to watch the foal being born," I said.

"Gerard, anytime you want to learn about what we do here or if you would simply like to come to watch the animals, please do not hesitate to visit us. You are always welcome here," said the farmer's wife.

"Thank you, I'm sure that I will take you up on your offer very soon. I really enjoyed the experience today," I answered.

"Here, my boy, I have a few more food items for Father Moyon! Please take them to him," and she gave me a large bag of fruit, vegetables and some homemade bread.

We shook hands and I started to walk toward the campsite. I was not tired but I had the presentiment that somehow I had been blessed. I felt peppy, as if a surge of energy had passed through my body and given me strength.

My day had been full. I had learnt a lot about astronomy, geography, and the cosmos and I had learned something about the facts of life as well! I was unhurt, lucky to be back from the spaceship. A thousand questions were going through my mind. Yet I was not ready to share my experiences with anyone.

As soon as I reached the camp I felt a sense of comfort and security. I still had butterflies in my stomach because I was afraid of the thousands of questions which might be thrown at me.

On the site, everything was hustle and bustle. Father Moyon was in the habit of dividing the tasks to be performed among various groups. Some were doing their daily chores, others were repairing and sewing tents and a large crew was cleaning the grounds and digging trenches around the perimeters of the site in case of rain. Father Moyon had always been very particular about sanitation, and rightly so. I was looking for Jose and Richard but did not see them.

Patrick came over and asked me if I had enjoyed watching the birth of the foal.

"How was it?"

"It was an experience, believe me," I answered.

"Yes? Jose and Richard told me that you had stayed behind to watch it, they said that the farmer's wife asked you to attend the birth," he said.

"Yes? That's true. There was a lot of blood; but the foal and the mare are both okay. The foal's name is Texas, like in the USA. The owner's wife is a nice woman. She has invited me to go back anytime I want to learn more about the animals."

"Good for you!" said Patrick.

"Have you seen Jose and Richard around?" I inquired.

"No, but when they came back from the farm, Father Moyon asked them to fetch some wood for the kitchen, so they went to the forest. I have not seen them since," he said.

"What's wrong, Gerard?" asked Patrick then. "You seem in a daze. Are you okay?"

"Nothing's wrong. I'm just tired, I guess," I replied. "I have to give these supplies to Father Moyon and check if he needs my help. Take care, Patrick! See you later."

I walked to the kitchen to find Father Moyon. It was situated in one of the largest marabouts in the camp. Grilling, steaming and roasting were done in a special area behind the main site. The chefs, city volunteers and students from the seminary were all employed in the preparation area, where we used coal and wood for the stoves.

Father Moyon placed the utmost emphasis on providing the camp's participants with the best cuisine. We had acquired several regional distinctions for it and numerous newspaper and magazine articles adorned the community centre's office walls, alongside notices about his standards of food management. Over the years, many parents and town business leaders had the chance to sample the menus offered to us. Descriptions like "sublime" and "fantastic" were quite common. As for us children, some even admitted that they ate better at the camp than at home.

"Sorry for being late," I said to Father Moyon. "I stayed to watch the birth of a foal and ..."

"Ah! Hello, Gerard! Don't worry," Father Moyon interjected. "I know about this already. Jose and Richard mentioned it to me. How was it? Did you learn anything?" He was smiling while taking the bag of food out of my arms.

"It was a memorable experience, the best science lesson that I've ever had, and I will never forget it," I answered.

"Yes, Gerard, God creates miracles with each birth. It does not matter if it relates to animals, men or insects. They are all the miracles of our maker," he said.

After witnessing a birth myself, I had to agree with him.

"Well, Gerard, why don't you give us a hand in the kitchen? We have bags of potatoes to peel. I have sent Jose and Richard to fetch some wood for the stoves, and they will be back soon. We need at least a full bag to be peeled for tonight. Thank you."

I took an apron and started to work. Father Moyon was discussing menus with the chefs and giving directives to the helpers and volunteers. I enjoyed these particular chores because the kitchen tent was always busy, animated and operational around the clock. Quite often, the cooks worked until the early hours in the morning preparing food for the next shift. Day or night, one could hear laughter and loud voices and smell the delicious aromas of the simmering dishes. It was a lot of fun to watch the liveliness and the considerable activities created by the barbeque ranges and the central kitchen. Whenever we could, we also used to come around the site to listen to the radio blaring out the most recent hits.

"Gerard, you are dreaming, my son!" Father Moyon exclaimed. He was standing in front of me with a frying pan in his hand, while I was holding a potato in my left and a knife in my right.

"Sorry, Father, you are right. It won't happen again!"

"No, it's okay Gerard, but the potatoes won't peel themselves, if you know what I mean!" he said laughingly.

I got back to work and tried to focus on what was taking place around me. It was difficult. Jose and Richard came back a little later with wood for the stoves. Both came over to meet me.

"Hello, Gerard, how was the foal?" they asked.

"Great, his name is Texas and both the mare and the foal are doing well," I answered.

Father Moyon came over and said: "Gerard witnessed today one of God's miracles. A birth. He saw it firsthand, and I know that it was better than any science class in school, wasn't it Gerard?" he asked.

"Yes, Father, a little hard to watch though, the blood and all. But it was amazing," I answered.

"You are right, amazing is the word for it, God performs miracles. Giving life to something is purely miraculous remember that," Father Moyon said.

"Now Jose, please go and help with the washing, Richard please join the others to dig some trenches. Gerard, keep up the speed on peeling those potatoes, otherwise they won't be cooked in time for dinner," he said. And everyone went about his duties.

I was observing everyone around me and as I was doing so my eyes rested on the clock which was attached in the kitchen on the main tent-pole. It showed 3:40pm As one of the seminarists passed by, I inquired about the time. He looked at his watch and answered, "3:40pm, Gerard!"

Eudoxus was correct. The time warp had materialized.

Everything had fallen into place. It was remarkable! It was really like a Hollywood movie!

I managed to finish my task on time. We would be able to eat mashed potatoes for dinner! Father Moyon was pleased at what I had done and gave me a short rest.

I left the kitchen and went into the woods nearby. I knelt on the ground and prayed. I remember asking Jesus for His help. I wanted to know what to do. Prayers do help a lot but we do not always receive what we ask for in them. That day however, He answered. I knew, deep inside my heart, that He had spoken to me and reached my soul. He gave me clear and precise instructions. He reassured me and I was finally relieved. After my prayers, I went back to the kitchen where Father Moyon was putting the final touches to the mashed potatoes.

CHAPTER EIGHT
FATHER MOYON'S INSIGHTS

Father Moyon was a true leader, highly respected by his entire team of volunteers and full-time employees. He had been my mentor for a few years and had always treated me properly. I enjoyed his coaching and, whenever I did something wrong, he would correct me without getting upset. He seldom raised his voice (unless it was in the tumultuous kitchen area). He was also a great motivator and insisted that we all perform to the best of our abilities. Young people had to try new things. To pursue a dream was an essential part of growing up. We all had dreams and Father Moyon urged us to talk about them openly, sometimes in groups or on a one-to-one basis if we preferred to do so. We also made mistakes and that was part of a learning process that Father Moyon understood. He used to say, "Those who do not make errors are those who do not do anything!" You could foul up as long as you were learning from it! He was a considerate person.

While preparing mashed potatoes he was also organizing weekly menus and timetables with the chefs and volunteers. I asked myself "How can he do so many things at once?" But he was relentless in his efforts to strive for perfection. It was part of his personality and he was a very dedicated and hard working priest. He used to refer to the recorded fact that the Emperor Napoleon could juggle seven tasks at once!

I asked him for a private meeting at the end of the day and he agreed to talk to me in the evening after the "roll-call". This assembly took place every evening after supper at 9pm

I went to see Jose and Richard who had completed their chores and we all went for a walk with our assigned groups. We enjoyed these promenades, during which we could exchange ideas, discuss the latest soccer scores and reminisce about the school year. The day at the camp was ending very nicely.

The roll-call was a very important part of the camp's daily life. For Father Moyon it was a way to maintain an open channel with the team (including the management) and the opportunity to discuss what went right or wrong with the daily chores, the site tours, the standards of cleanliness or any other organized activities. In addition, this gathering enabled him to pray with his "family" and sometimes to express his dissatisfaction or contentment regarding any particular situation at the camp. All had to attend without exception.

I can mention that some of these assemblies were very heated! Father Moyon was the type of person who would tell things the way they were. He would not hide his opinions behind his priest's robes. That is why he held a general meeting daily, in front of everyone, following the roll-call. Not behind closed doors, but in the open, "in full view of the Lord", as he said. At all times he remained polite with all of us.

His great sense of humour would also emerge from time to time and we would all laugh together.

A few of Father Moyon's methods were almost military in nature. Above all he loved sports. By combining strict discipline with sports he could make us understand, not only that he was the camp's ultimate boss, but also that a healthy mind lives in a healthy body. If we had to be punished for small infractions during the course of the day, Father Moyon would wait for the roll-call and then he would make us do one hundred push-ups, jumping jacks, sit-ups, etc. It was great exercise before going to bed!

Prior to assembling together we regularly took a short walk after supper. On that particular night, as I went around the campsite, looking at the sky, watching the stars, and admiring the moon, I just could not stop wondering what Eudoxus was doing at that moment. Was he on Toki, or flying around the universe?

Father Moyon was in a great mood at the roll-call. He thanked everyone for a job well done with the daily chores and he officially introduced the chefs, the new seminarists and volunteers who were working in the kitchen. We did not get reprimanded and we did fifty push ups just for the fun of it.

At 9:30pm I went to meet him at the central tent. He listened to me attentively when I talked about the UFO phenomenon and my interest in space research and astronomy. I saw him smile when I brought up the topic of space kidnappings and also when I invited his opinions regarding "close encounters versus religion." As a matter of fact, I was not sure at that time that I should bring up the question. But he was a priest and his insights were of the utmost importance to me, particularly in view of the controversial messages propagated by the media. Many seemed simply ridiculous and without foundation.

I believed in God and at that particular time I needed some clarity. I felt that by talking to Father Moyon I would regain my peace of mind. He was pleased that I had come to him for advice.

He told me that my interest in astronomy, space research and UFOs was praiseworthy. He himself believed that in our galaxy – and there were maybe many more, he added – other living forms could easily exist. Why should we be alone? He had not particularly studied the subject, but he always kept an open mind, and he had found that the press, Hollywood movies, and the public at large did not really have the true facts. He was aware of the adverse effects of such movies and press coverage on the general population because, after all, there was absolutely no proof that aliens had done us any harm whatsoever. Father Moyon admitted that his knowledge of astronomy and his interest in space research were both very limited. He believed that our planet would one day be over-populated and that we would have to find new environments to accommodate all of us. Father Moyon told me that there were only two ways of achieving this. One was, "A new habitat in space or on other planets," and the other was, "Possibly below sea level." Looking back, I can see that he was correct.

He also spoke about the frescoes of tall blond men wearing long white robes, arguably carrying rockets on their backs, which have been found at religious sites around the world, and what some publications have said about these. He mentioned the strange characters and symbols that have been found in certain temples, churches, caves and grottoes, and some popular journalists' claims that these are messages from the gods beyond. Magazines and newspapers have to sell their products, he said, and sometimes they print anything to achieve the necessary sales. "Frankly speaking, Gerard," he said, "Do you really believe that God, Jesus and Mary are aliens with rockets on their backs, flying around performing miracles? Are angels, the soldiers of our Lord Jesus, propelled by jet turbines under their wings?"

"No, Father," I answered, "these theories seem rather foolish to me."

"You are correct Gerard," Father Moyon said. "God created the entire universe and its beauties but that does not make him an alien. The Lord is watching us at all times and I know that He pays particular attention to scientific breakthroughs. He wants them to benefit world peace and not cause wars. The Virgin Mary, Jesus and the angels protect us. They help our Father. None of them are people from outer space! Such assertions are ludicrous.

"We are thinking of going into space, but we still do not know what is happening on Earth! We have not yet fully explored our oceans, our jungles, our mountains. Once again, we are riding a bicycle before walking. This is typical of humankind," he said.

"However, Gerard," he continued, "space research has tremendous benefits. It is the lifeline to our survival."

On the subject of close encounters and space kidnappings Father Moyon was more cautious. He said that all sightings should be investigated by formal agencies prior to being confirmed. Too many charlatans had become involved with the phenomena, creating damaging hoaxes, so that the public at large had become more reluctant to believe in the authenticity of peaceful aliens visiting Earth.

It was late and we were very tired. Before we parted, Father Moyon asked me: "Even though you are passionate about this issue, did something happen today that compelled this meeting?"

"No Father, I only needed your input to shed light on some questions that were nagging me, that's all," I replied.

My response did not sound very convincing and he looked at me strangely.

As I was leaving the kitchen he suggested that I contact the local office of the gendarmerie to request information about UFO incidents.

I assured him that I would follow up on it as soon as the summer camp was over.

It was finally the end of that very hectic Thursday and I slept like a log.

In France we have a saying: "A good night's sleep brings sound advice to the mind."

CHAPTER NINE
MY SECOND ENCOUNTER

The following day I woke up in a great mood and I decided to carry on during the rest of the summer as if nothing had happened. It was an excellent decision, because the remainder of the summer camp went beautifully.

Jose, Richard, Patrick and I had a lot of fun and Father Moyon made sure that all the planned activities were completed to the T. They included water-rafting, swimming, mountain-climbing, hiking, soccer and working in local vineyards. I also went back to the farm because the owner had carved out time from her busy schedule to teach me how to milk a cow, feed the cattle and to shear lambs. It made me realize that life on a farm is very hard work and that not everybody is made for it.

School time was approaching fast and I returned home in a great frame of mind. I was tanned, rested and ready to start eighth grade.

When I went to see the gendarmes, regarding details about UFO activities in Southern France, the captain in charge gave me the cold shoulder. He categorically refused to discuss it, insisting that the documents in the "French Blue Book" were of a "classified nature" and "official national security evidence." He was smiling when he told me this, probably because he thought that a twelve year old kid had no business discussing UFOs.

I was unsuccessful in my query but at least I had tried.

For the next three years I kept studying very hard, practised my sports and joined the local boy scouts. I read about space research and astronomy but I could not get substantial information about UFOs.

In those days spacecraft and aliens were subjects only for movies and for lunatics who believed in their existence.

My parents were not interested in discussing it with me and probably thought that my passion was merely temporary. In the late 1950s, public libraries were not much help in my UFO research. I was forced to content myself with collecting newspaper articles about the odd sighting, because these were the only sources of information that I had.

I did not find anyone who shared my interest but it did not matter. I had experienced a close encounter and no one could change that.

Once in a while, I thought about Eudoxus and I knew deep inside my heart that we would meet again. Patience is a virtue and I was waiting patiently for more proofs of Eudoxus' knowledge and the capabilities of the Mathesus stone.

The boy scouts had given me a new perspective in life. I enjoyed the discipline, the camaraderie, and also the learning experiences. In addition, it was very demanding physically and I was always ready for new challenges.

I thought that it would give me a very good preparation for my military service and also that I could learn some survival techniques as well.

Our local branch ran weekend trips and summer camps. It was during one of those outings that my second encounter with Eudoxus took place. It was the spring of 1962 and our team leader had arranged a three day trip near Dam François Zola, one of the largest dams in the region.

I was fifteen years old, in great physical shape and loved the outdoors...

CHAPTER TEN
THE ACCIDENT

Two highly trained scout leaders joined us on this excursion in order to review all the techniques that we had learnt about survival and escalade.

They were extremely knowledgeable and were going to drive home the importance of safety measures. At the end of the first day, we were told of a night exercise of the utmost importance. It combined all the necessary challenges and components for those who completed it successfully to gain the award of the coveted "survival badge". It was a top reward for a boy scout.

Our small group was very experienced. We were divided into four teams, and our instructor made sure that we had received our supplies and first aid kits. Each group was also given a compass and a briefing prior to leaving the camp. We were warned that it was a new site for this test, and that it would be difficult. However, we were not to worry about getting lost, as our guides already knew the region. We were all expected to perform very well.

We left our base camp and walked along a ten mile track toward a large plateau which overlooked a dam and its artificial lake. That night, there was no full moon and it was cloudy. As a result, it was pitch black. In the silent environment we could hear the thundering sound of the water spurting out of the turbines in the power plant located at the bottom of the barrage.

There was a resonant echo throughout the valley. This, added to the fact that we were not familiar with this rugged terrain and its surroundings, made us a little bit nervous.

Our leader, Valia Vourias, carried a torch to be used only in case of emergency, as we were supposed to move in the dark, finding direction only by using a compass and our personal sense of orientation.

"Let's go down now, Boys," he said.

We slowly descended through bushes, small pine trees, mounds of gravel and grassy knolls. It was very steep and we were holding on to anything we could in order not to fall down the hill. Soon we arrived at the top of a chimney.

I had completed this type of challenge before and this one seemed standard for its degree of difficulty. It measured approximately fifteen metres in vertical length but was very narrow at the top. We had to begin by climbing down the outside, until we reached halfway down the shaft and then we were to move inside. After that it would be easy. We should just follow the sinuous path down to the bottom.

We had not brought a rope with us, relying only on our expertise gained through training. Our instructor went down first. We asked him, when it was our turn, to help us by shining his torch. We attentively observed every step to be taken. I tried to retain in my mind where my hands and feet had to be placed. Our instructor was an expert and reached the base of the chimney very quickly. I was next and it proved more complicated than I had thought. I struggled with the smooth surface of the rock. But once I was inside the passage, it all went well. The two other scouts were quicker than me and demonstrated outstanding skill. The four of us were now standing on a small platform overlooking a very dense forest. Our leader moved his torch to the side illuminating our next challenge. It was a precipice, a twelve-metre-high wall of stone. We were told that it was easy to handle even though it was abrupt.

There were a lot of indentations and crevasses from top to bottom along the cliff. Our guide gave us final instructions prior to undertaking the next phase of the test.

We had to maintain a straight descent because at the foot of the obstacle was a very narrow footpath going through the forest. It was essential not to miss this footpath in the darkness. Once on it, we were to follow it, jogging and walking as fast as possible. Without the benefit of any light we had to go all around the very highly elevated mountain and come back to the plateau surmounting the dam. We would be timed by the instructor along the way. The exercise combined escalade, courage, orientation abilities and endurance. We had to handle the two routes, up and down the elevations, to base camp. We were also convinced that another challenge would be waiting for us upon our arrival, but we did not know for sure.

The first scout went down the cliff without any difficulty. He used the grooves in the rock to his advantage. I was next and hoped to do better than the last time. I struggled but eventually made it. I was still quite slow and hesitated too much when positioning my hands and feet into the crevasses. I was starting to feel that escalade was not my forte. The third member of the group once more performed his test without any complications. Our monitor had coached us, and helped us to maintain a straight descent so that we would not miss the footpath. He was undeniably a motivator and a good leader.

From the bottom of the precipice the three of us looked up as our instructor prepared to join us on the path. He turned off his torch, attached it to his belt and started to descend.

Suddenly he lost his grip and fell backwards. We heard a loud scream and watched in awe as his body crashed into the trees.

There were many cracking sounds as branches broke, followed by two long screams and then a dead silence.

We looked at each other, petrified, for a few seconds and then rushed into the woods.

We knew that he could not have landed very far away, but it was so dark that it made finding him difficult. We inspected the ground, checked thoroughly inside the low bushes, and one of the scouts even climbed a tree to have a better view of the site. There was no trace of Valia. There was one positive aspect of the accident, this scout found. The edge of the forest came right to the bottom of the cliff. Thus, it seemed that Valia would not have hit rocks or the ground at full speed when he fell. – He had just begun his descent when for no apparent reason he fell backwards into the forest. – We hoped that the vegetation and the wild brush had somehow broken his fall.

The darkness was a real handicap. We were afraid to move too far into the woods in case we got lost. Even worse, we could lose sight of the trail and that would have devastating consequences. So we stayed close to each other and kept moving in ever-widening circles, looking for Valia as we had been trained to do during the search and rescue drills.

One of the scouts named Alain suddenly shouted: "There, I see him on the right, look!"

One metre above the ground, in the thickness of the lower branches of a very large tree, Valia's body was suspended like a scarecrow.

He was not moving, his arms and legs dangled, his head was pushed back, his eyes were closed and his chest seemed motionless. We were not even sure if he was breathing.

In the shadows of the dense vegetation surrounding us this tragic scene was almost grotesque.

We called his name loudly, hoping to revive consciousness in him, but without result.

Approaching close, I took the torch from his belt and paced slowly around him trying to evaluate his condition.

Apart from the torch, he also carried a safety kit. But it was small and very basic, not of any use in this case. We were facing a major accident which had caused internal bleeding and perhaps, death.

I moved the light up and down his entire body and noticed that his skin was white. He was cold and sweaty with blood coming out of his ears and mouth. He had a lot of scratches on his face from the fall and I was worried that maybe he had broken his neck or his back when hitting the trees.

There were no visible open fractures on his arms or legs.

"Is he dead, Gerard?" asked Alain.

"I must check his breathing. Pass me the safety kit and please let's not move him at all. He may have a broken spine or a broken neck. Go easy," I answered.

We untied the backpack from his shoulders very slowly.

I pulled out a small mirror and placed it close to his mouth. I saw a little bit of fog forming on the glass and I yelled: "Yes, he's alive, but he's very, very weak. I don't know if he will be alive for long. It's critical!"

"Look at his right shoulder and left side, Gerard! What is it?" asked the other scout, Didi.

Valia was wearing a thick sweater and I placed the torch above the two areas Didi had mentioned. I had not noticed anything unusual on my first inspection.

"Oh no!" I exclaimed.

Two branches had pierced right through his body, entering from one side and exiting at the other. They were protruding, but blood was not spurting out of the wounds. It was a miracle that Valia was still alive.

"Gerard, what do we do now?" inquired Alain.

"Well, we cannot move him at all; we must leave the branches in the wounds to avoid any hæmorraging. He is alive but comatose. It's very desperate. We must get help at once!

"I shall stay here with him," I decided. "You two, take the trail, follow it to the base camp, use your whistles to call an SOS every five minutes on your way up. There are four or five other teams in the area near the dam. They will hear you. Our chief at the lodge has a car and a radio monitor. Make sure that he calls the fire department and the gendarmes. They will send the proper rescue teams to help us. If you run fast, we still might save Valia's life.

"I will also call an SOS every five minutes with my whistle and I will use the torch as well. Someone will see it, it has a powerful battery, and it can last for hours.

"Now you guys, please go; and good luck!"

Didi and Alain both took off, running like hell.

CHAPTER ELEVEN
SAVING VALIA

Time was of the essence and I knew that Alain and Didi were going to run up the hill with all their might to save Valia.

Meanwhile, I had to keep him alive and breathing, until rescue arrived. He must have been in terrible pain, but he had not moved nor spoken a word. His wounds were not bleeding profusely, but they had undoubtedly caused very serious internal damages.

He was at intervals responding feebly and his chest was slowly rising. He was a fighter and I was asking the Lord to make him better.

I kept talking to him just in case he regained consciousness, but to no avail.

Valia fell into a deep coma and, at that stage, I could do no more for him. It was extremely frustrating. I had sent four SOS signals in a short time, including two with my torch, but I had received no immediate response. However, I trusted that these signals had been picked up by other teams. We were all testing and perfecting our skills in the same sector.

"Prayer is very powerful and effective," Father Moyon used to say.

That night, I prayed a lot because I wanted Valia to survive his horrific ordeal. He was a good young man. As time passed, I slowly felt more and more helpless, just waiting by his side and, as it seemed, watching him die.

I went down on my knees and prayed with all my heart. I talked aloud to Mary, to my guardian angels, to Jesus himself and to God the Almighty. I begged them all for support, for mercy and healing for Valia. What could I do to be more useful, I asked in my prayers? Did I do the right thing in this emergency?

Suddenly a bright and large beam of light came down from above. It illuminated a large area around me, including Valia's body, the cliff and the forest around us. I immediately thought that it was a rescue helicopter, but there was no sound.

The ray of light was warm, and getting brighter. It continued circling, probing and covering the entire stretch of the forest, moving up and down the trail.

I tried to look up but its intensity was too powerful.

"Hello Gerard, it seems that you need my help tonight!"

I recognized that voice immediately. It was Eudoxus!

I was still on my knees. There he was, standing beside Valia's body.

I got up and we shook hands. Eudoxus had not changed at all, he was still wearing an immaculate white jump suit, white robe, and red boots, with the Mathesus stone on his belt. His long blond hair covered his shoulders and he seemed as calm as when we had met before.

I started to explain. "Eudoxus, my leader is badly hurt, he fell from the cliff over there and branches have pierced his body. My team has gone to look for rescue teams, but I do not know if Valia will be able to wait that long."

"No, he cannot wait much longer, Gerard," said Eudoxus. "He's dying. His internal bleeding has increased and he suffered tremendous shock and trauma; besides, his neck has been broken in the fall, and the injuries have taken a toll on his heart. Luckily, he is strong and young, otherwise he would have passed away already."

"Can you do something to save him, Eudoxus?" I asked.

"That is why I am here, Gerard," he answered. You prayed for help. Someone heard you and help has materialized. Now, let's be quick or your friend won't live to see another day."

Eudoxus placed his left hand on Valia's chest and his right on the Mathesus stone which covered the buckle of his belt. He closed his eyes and there was silence. Suddenly I heard a whistling sound and the ray of light above us became hotter. Its brilliance intensified and it enveloped all of us as if we were in a whirlwind.

Unexpectedly we all rose from the ground, lifted up rapidly in a standing posture.

Because of my previous experience with Eudoxus, I was not afraid. I was curious about the treatment that Valia was about to receive.

I heard a big *clung* noise. A door had opened. It became pitch black all around us. We were now inside the flying-saucer where

Eudoxus took charge immediately. I heard him talk to people in a language that I could not identify.

I was still in darkness and I had not moved. I was not sure which area of the spaceship I had entered.

"Eudoxus, can you give me some light please, I can't move!" I asked.

"Not yet, wait a little while, Gerard," answered Eudoxus. "Stay where you are. I will come and get you in a few minutes."

Emergency lights started to appear around the ceiling. Then Eudoxus came back and informed me as follows: "You are on an experimental and research vessel. It was commissioned from our mother-ship to rescue your friend.

"Valia is going into surgery and I expect him to recuperate fully. Do not worry. He is going to survive. He has been examined and the prognosis is very good. You may come and watch through this window."

We walked through a door into a different area. The room where we were now standing was very well lit. I followed Eudoxus to what appeared to be the surgical block. It was incredibly bright inside and a group of four doctors dressed in blue uniforms were hastily working on Valia.

They were all wearing masks, so I could not see their faces. Definitely they were smaller than Eudoxus. They may have been one and a half metres tall at the most. I could not comprehend a word of what they were saying for they communicated with high pitched noises, sounding like little birds.

Eudoxus told me that they were the surgeons on board the craft and that they were highly trained in emergency medicine.

"Eudoxus, they look very different from you," I said. "Are they also from Toki?"

"No, Gerard, they are not. They travel with us, they help us. Some of them live on our planet, but originally they came from a different part of the galaxy. They are very advanced in all technologies, medicine, and studies of the human species. They are actually very gentle and caring people.

"Now, Gerard, I am going to make a final check on your friend Valia, before he is released back to you." As he said this, Eudoxus pressed buttons on a coloured panel and entered the operating unit.

I was observing attentively the proceedings inside the module and I noticed how sparkling clean everything was. This was logical as it was an operating theatre, but it looked different from any other hospital or surgical block that I had seen before.

It was spartan, containing almost no equipment, and there was a very intense and constant brightness all over the room. I could see no wires, no side tables, no consoles. The doctors did not handle scalpels or scissors. There were no machines, no breathing apparatus, nothing. Eudoxus was now wearing a blue surgical uniform like the other doctors. He was in charge and he was asking questions of the group while discussing some charts. I could see Valia's body lying on a long white table; he was wearing a hood on his head to which coloured tubes were connected. Around his chest, a very wide grey belt had been strapped, to which many coloured tubes had also been attached. He was naked, but his skin looked much better than before. Eudoxus performed a complete examination from head to toe.

The coloured tubes were all connected to medium-size cylinders made of some lustrous element which was fastened to the wall behind Valia's operating table.

Eudoxus removed Valia's hood and checked his vitals and his neck, then he took off the chest belt and made sure that Valia was breathing normally. There were no scars at all on Valia's chest! Two wooden sticks had gone through his body and they had not left any marks! How could that be?

Then Valia's body was turned on his stomach and the surgeons inserted some golden needles into his spine and neck. About ten minutes later they applied the same treatment to his chest, his abdomen and again to his neck. This style of therapy was known to me as acupuncture and is of Chinese origin. It is thousands of years old. I was quite surprised to see it used by such an advanced civilization! Within fifteen minutes the needles were removed and Eudoxus lowered the lighting in the operating room. I could still distinguish the team around the naked body of the patient and saw a Mathesus stone placed on his heart. Then they all took a step back.

The gem began to scintillate and rapidly switched colours. It went from bright red to pink to orange and then back to red. A large golden aura formed above the operating table and glittered all over the room.

Valia looked much better and had regained his colour. He seemed to be sleeping soundly. He did not have a single mark on his body. Eudoxus moved the team against the back wall, opened a small partition and pressed some buttons. After a few seconds, the radiance in the block increased and a spectacular scene took place.

It was as if the room had suddenly gone wild, producing a storm without any rain. Blue and purple lightning flashes were cracking everywhere. All lights shut off. Rambunctious noises detonated all over it.

I noticed that a perfectly-formed white halo was hovering above Valia. I sensed a connection between the lightning flashes, the electricity in the air, the halo and the Mathesus stone. They were feeding each other and all their energies were channelled into the stone reposing on Valia Vourias' body which absorbed them all.

The electric rays, the powerful energies and the vibrant currents contained in the room were all visible, and created a very spooky atmosphere. The halo floating above Valia was emanating with a very forceful magnetism and the blue light was being pulled into the Mathesus stone.

Next, Eudoxus and his team turned Valia back onto his stomach and repeated the treatment. This time the gem was placed at the bottom of his spine. I could see a turn in his condition. He was recovering quickly and his muscles were moving under the effect of the intense electrodes.

Once this second treatment was completed, one of the doctors pressed the Mathesus stone on vital areas of Valia's body. He moved it from the head, the neck, the thorax, and the lower abdomen, to the legs and feet. Then a set of clean clothes was brought in.

They all left the room. The ceiling lights came back on. Classical music became heard in the unit.

Eudoxus approached me. "Gerard," he said, "Valia is fine. He's healthy again. His internal organs have been checked and healed. His broken bones have also been fixed. It was very serious. He will be tired for about two days, but he is now in full recovery, thanks to you!" said Eudoxus.

"No, Eudoxus! You and your team did it all. Your science is so advanced that it is even scary. Look, I am totally baffled at what I saw here!"

"Yes Gerard, I understand that you are astonished at this type of surgical intervention. You saw our team in action, utilizing very unusual devices and a type of swift treatment that we use only in cases of extreme emergency.

"The application of the Mathesus stone has given Valia back his energy and strength. We revitalized two major organs, his kidneys and his liver. We pulled two wooden sticks out of his body, then cauterized the wounds. We never leave any scars after surgery. Valia's heart is strong. The electrical forces revived his muscles and brought his blood pressure under control."

I suddenly noticed two little creatures going into the operating block and begin to dress Valia. They were one and a half metres tall at the most. Their skin was grey and wrinkled in certain parts of their bodies. Their ears, mouths, and noses were slits. I could not understand their language, but Eudoxus could communicate with them. Each of their hands and feet bore four long digits only. They talked very quickly, emitting a chirping kind of noise. Their black eyes were oval with no eyelids. Their movements were prompt and methodical.

They carried Valia to another part of the ship. Eudoxus assured me that one day we would sit down together again, and that I would be able to ask him questions relating to Toki, the Mathesus stone and his visits to Earth. But right now, Valia's rescue was a priority.

But I still had one question for Eudoxus.

Eudoxus had praised me for not giving Valia anything to drink and also trying to keep him awake while wounded. He had given me all the details regarding the surgery and Valia's recovery status. I asked him about his timely arrival on Earth to save Valia's life. All he could say was that a "voice" had called him and that he had to come immediately.

"I was commanded, Gerard, that is all I can say. You saved Valia, Gerard, you did it for him, and it was your prayers that started the action.

"The power of prayer is unparalleled. You asked for help and the Lord of the Universe did the rest. We had the science, the ability and the right manpower to save him and we acted upon it with urgency.

"Because it was a matter of life and death, the team concentrated all their efforts on bringing the victim back to life and making him better. We succeeded in doing so. Once again, I apologize for not staying longer, but your friend needs to go to hospital to rest. I will beam you both out on the top of the plateau, where you can easily be found. Please keep signaling with your torch and whistling to attract attention and get people to come."

I was extremely relieved that Valia had been saved and very happy to have seen Eudoxus again. We would meet further no doubt and hopefully in less stressful circumstances.

Strange sounds came from behind me. Someone was running and talking in a very odd way. The little grey men were already cleaning and preparing the surgical block for the next patient. Others were getting Valia ready for transportation.

I spoke to Eudoxus about my concern: "Please Eudoxus, I am extremely worried about what to say about this recovery. Didi and Alain were with me when Valia hurt himself. We were all at the bottom of the cliff and saw that branches were coming out of his chest while he was suspended in the trees. He was comatose, all bloody, and his clothes torn to shreds. He was almost dead and could not speak nor move a finger. Now, what am I going to say to everyone? What should I answer to any questions the police or the ambulance drivers may ask me? Also, Didi and Alain will never understand how Valia could move from his original position and make it to the plateau wearing a clean uniform and showing no scars on his body. What am I going to say or do? Please give me a hint!"

Eudoxus looked at me with the same expression and the same smile on his face as three years previously, after the spaceship landing.

"Do not concern yourself with these details. Didi and Alain will not even discuss Valia's wounds. The rescue teams are very anxious to find you both at the present time. They have been searching everywhere, on the trail, down the cliff, on the top of the dam, up the hill and they will find you on the plateau.

"Valia is alive and well and so are you. You will be praised for your efforts and courage. It is well deserved since you have not only been very brave, but also calm and collected throughout the ordeal. Great work! Now it is time to move on. Please follow me onto the transportation deck and stay with Valia. It will not take long.

"I shall see you in the future, Gerard. I promise you that we shall communicate at a later date. It might take longer than we would like, but it will certainly happen."

I did not have time to reply as a large door closed behind me, followed by a very bright purple light illuminating the deck.

The platform where we stood was made of a dark metallic material and there was a large red circle at the centre where Valia's body had been placed.

"Please stand beside Valia," a voice commanded.

I moved close to Valia, and noticed that he was still asleep, but looking much healthier. He had no marks or traces of having been hurt. He even looked much cleaner than I was after all the tribulations I had gone through. A long strident whistling sound began, followed by extremely powerful lights. The beams were switching from blue to purple to incandescent white.

It felt like the room was rotating around us, but it was too bright to see anything. I heard a *clung* noise and we were going downward. Valia and I were wrapped in a purple and blue ray of light.

We touched down onto the ground, softly.

CHAPTER TWELVE
SOS! SOS! SOS!

The extraction from the UFO had taken only a few minutes. I looked up and saw a very large crown of light above me. I heard a high-pitched sound, combined with some coloured illuminations which were dancing from left to right and up and down. Then all the lights went out. Suddenly a deafening blast burst into the darkness of the night. The spaceship had disappeared. It was gone. It was all over. Looking at the sky, I could not stop wondering at such technological power. In the 1960s, there was no plane on Earth able to follow the UFOs. It was beyond imagination. The speed of the UFO was phenomenal.

Then I heard some voices at a distance. I immediately blew my whistle, signalling SOS! SOS! SOS! I also took the torch from my belt and sent some more messages signaling a crisis. I must have alerted other teams because I could hear the sounds of engines and shouting, moving closer and closer to my location. I turned on the light one more time. I signaled, "Help, Help", and then I yelled, "Here! Here! I'm here!"

Someone responded, "Hey, I see them, we've found them! Quick, bring the rescue team over here!"

Within a few seconds, I was surrounded by boy scouts, chief scouts, emergency personnel and gendarmes.

Valia's condition was checked and he was transported to base camp where an ambulance took him to the city's hospital for observation.

A lot of energy had been spent that night trying to find us and now everyone was relieved that we were both alive and well.

I saw a police helicopter flying low over the dam, and the local detachment of gendarmes patrolling the area on foot and with jeeps.

Didi and Alain had really done a great job, informing everyone of the incident. I was told later that they met a team while climbing the side of the hill. As one of the leaders was carrying a portable radio, they were able to call base camp and start the search immediately. They notified the police, the firefighters and the EMS (Emergency Medical Services) as well. A rescue alert had immediately been put into motion.

I had to answer a lot of questions pertaining to the accident, but afterwards I was driven home for a good night's rest.

My parents were happy for Valia and they were proud of me. I had saved someone's life.

The following week was hectic. I had to write a report describing the event and what I did to keep Valia alive. Didi and Alain's reports did not coincide accurately with mine regarding his chest wounds. I had expected that much, anyway. However, since there were absolutely no traces on his body, the authorities assumed that both my partners made an error because of the frantic situation at the time of the fall.

The doctors were amazed that Valia had not incurred any serious injury. He had suffered only mild concussion and shock.

Valia did not remember very much about his fall.

He was, however, thankful to be alive, and he wanted to rest for a while. He told us his version of the story, and we learnt that, as he was going down the cliff, a piece of rock broke off from under his right foot, causing him to lose his grip.

He recalled falling backward, but everything had gone blank after that.

Valia's parents thanked us profusely for saving their son's life, and it was an emotional experience. A few days later, we all attended a ceremony in full boy-scout uniform to receive the "survival badges". Many parents were present and we were given a lot of praise for our actions. We had made the scouts and our families very proud. Meantime, I had some "face to face" discussions with Didi and Alain, pertaining to the injuries sustained on that night by Valia.

It was very hard for me, because I could not reveal Eudoxus' existence and I was not able to produce any evidence either. In my heart we owed it all to him, and I was embarrassed not to be able to disclose that fact to anyone.

I told Didi and Alain that I had carried Valia up the hill after realizing that his injuries were not as serious as they had appeared to be.

Just by looking at their faces I could see that they did not believe me but after some persuasion they had decided to drop the subject.

Eudoxus had been right again. It had ended very well. Valia had been saved, nobody ever knew that strangers from another planet had used their advanced medical skills to operate on him. And finally, I had managed to provide sufficient and satisfactory explanations to the inquiry and the authorities.

In addition, the three of us looked like heroes. Eventually I stayed one more year with the scouts as an assistant leader.

It would be another two years before Eudoxus reappeared in my life.

CHAPTER THIRTEEN
CAREER OPTIONS

It was 1963 and I had been a good student at the Lycée Mignet in Aix-en-Provence. But somehow I was restless and, like all teenagers, I had dreams.

Times were different then. Money was scarce at home. I wanted to become a surgeon but it was out of the question because my parents would never have been able to pay for my education and my expenses for the twelve years study required to become qualified. I also wanted to travel, see other countries and learn English.

On the other hand, a career in the military was tempting and my family was open to the latter.

The question was, what branch of the military should I choose?

What were my options? What specialty could I choose, which would allow me to reintegrate to civilian life at a later date? My father raised some of these questions and I planned to investigate it further with the army office.

There was also the opportunity to go to work in the restaurant business and climb that particular career ladder. A career in the hospitality industry would enable me to travel all around the world if I wanted to. I liked that idea very much.

Over the next few weeks, I did some serious investigating regarding my two career options: the military or the restaurant industry. My father was not very happy about it because he had higher hopes for his son's future.

I was a very good student and my wish to leave school at that time was for him incomprehensible.

In any case, I felt trapped in an environment that I loathed and I was in a rut. School was still enjoyable but I was bored to death with my home-life. I had become frustrated with the daily routine. Watching my parents struggling financially, with no ambitions of their own, annoyed me tremendously. I found my entire surroundings suffocating. I wanted to travel, move around and see the world. I had big dreams; but to achieve them, I had to get out of town, so to speak. Firstly, I spoke with military officers about opportunities with the navy, the air force and the airborne regiments. I also read novels and brochures about the French commandos and finally asked advice from friends of mine who were older and had already completed their national service.

Then I inquired about the restaurant business from some former school buddies who had dropped out and were working full time at local cafés and restaurants. They all agreed on several points. The hours were long. The work was strenuous. The discipline was intense. And the job required a lot of energy. At first the money would not be great. The length of the training period would vary according to the style of the operation and one's ability to grasp all the techniques. Because I would have to work on holidays, over weekends and the various special events throughout the year, my social life would totally evaporate. It was, in fact, a tough career to contemplate. To survive through the first years, my friends recommended that there would have to be a very serious change of lifestyle habits.

I asked my father also about the pros and cons of entering the *métier*. I was more interested in the service side than the kitchen. I had never aspired to become a *chef de cuisine*.

My goal was to learn English and possibly move up the ladder while travelling in order to reach the position of *maître d'hôtel*.

Many arguments took place at home, but the debates did eventually come to an end because the final decision was mine. In the summer of 1963, I started work as a bar boy and bus boy in the restaurant at the Hôtel du Roi René in Aix-en-Provence. I was now sixteen years old.

In spite of this, a military career was of course still open to me if I wanted to pursue it, because I could either enlist voluntarily at the age of eighteen, or decide to stay in the force at the end of my mandatory national service.

My father was a concierge at the same establishment, which was ranked among the best in the country by the coveted Michelin Guide.

It was a four star deluxe hotel, and with its one "gastronomic star" restaurant was the jewel of the city. Mr Charles Guillon, the general manager, controlled the operation with an iron hand.

The job was interesting and challenging, and I enjoyed meeting the most famous people in the world. In those days, the hotel was considered an important institution, a renowned retreat for movie stars, entertainers, politicians and the "who's who" within the high society of Europe and America. Some guests stayed there on their way to the French Riviera while others stayed with us on their way back to Paris on business. Aix-en-Provence was a staging point in their journey and this magnificent hostelry gave them all the privacy that they required, plus top-notch service. They could relax incognito far away from the media. Later on in my career I would meet many of the same personalities in London, Montreal, and Toronto.

The hours were as grueling as I had been told to expect. We would work weeks at a time without any days off, particularly in the summer months.

Occasionally, I was sent to help at the company's other operations. *La Société du Casino d'Aix-en-Provence* owned the two major hotels in town, L'Hôtel du Roi René and l'Hôtel des Thermes, as well as a two-star Michelin Guide restaurant called Le Vendôme. I went to each of these locations from time to time, whenever they needed my help. Eventually, I took up a full time position at "Le Vendôme", where I received the best training of my career.

I worked such long hours that my social life was reduced to almost nothing. To describe my time more accurately it was work, sleep, work, sleep. I had been pre-warned and I never complained about it. Every so often, I did have a cup of coffee with a colleague at a local bistro during my afternoon breaks. The restaurant business is definitely a tough business. We mainly worked on a split shift schedule and I used any spare time I did have to study English or swim at the local pool. At the end of the season, the *maitre d'hôtel* gave us a week's holiday to relax in, before we began a new programme of festivities, beginning from the month of October and continuing to January of the following year.

With my family, I went to the seaside. The place was called Le Grau du Roi, a charming little fishing town in the South of France.

It was renowned for its deserted sand beaches, historical expeditions, sailing, fishing, scuba diving and deep sea fishing and above all, its casual lifestyle. My father and I went out angling every day, fishing for red snappers, eels, and sea bass. On some occasions, we were even invited by the local fishermen to catch sardines, tuna, swordfish, octopus and various other species from the Mediterranean Sea. Regularly, large shoals of mackerel would swim up the main stream and get caught in the main canal. There we would hook them with our long special homemade rods and have a wonderful supper! My Dad taught me to look for larger catches at night. It meant positioning ourselves at the entrance to the harbour, down at the bottom of the pier, very close to the water. It was often windy, wet and cold. However uncomfortable it was though, we regularly stayed out there from 10pm to 6am without taking a break. The results of our endeavours were abundant and the hotel chef had fun cooking for us. These were great times for our family!

CHAPTER FOURTEEN
ENTER THE GHOST

During these wonderful holidays I also ate raw fish for the first time.

The locals always had breakfast very early on their boats at sea. If their catch had been above expectation, they would even include hard liquor or some wine.

I was taught to clean and eat sardines, eels, and small octopus, served with freshly baked bread and a glass of cold white wine or cognac at five or six in the morning. I still have fond memories of those times.

Le Grau du Roi was in a very picturesque location, with two tall lighthouses guarding the entrance to the harbour. The town consisted of a large canal, flanked on each side by long piers. A large mobile bridge was located in the centre of town. All along the moles, heavy rocks and cement blocks had been placed for support and protection. When the sun was high in the azure blue sky and all the colourful fishing boats were aligned in the port, it made ideal scenery for a picture postcard.

On the left-hand side of the piers, a large gulf was separated by two peninsulas of white sand beaches, the sites of new condominiums, deluxe hotels and pricey real estate. Le Grau du Roi was already on its way to prosperity as a fruitful fishing port and tourist centre.

On the right-hand side of the piers, on the edge of town, a small road led to the most beautiful beaches one could ever imagine. There was nothing like it anywhere else in the entire country. I never saw anyone swimming or sunbathing there, but there was a rumour that nudists took advantage of the solitude. This particular part of the resort was called The Sahara because of the sand dunes, gigantic hills of golden sand spreading for miles and miles along the coastline.

Walking by myself along the seashore with the hot sand under my feet was very relaxing. All I could hear was the sound of the waves rolling in on the sand, and the cries of the seagulls. To reach the beach, one had to cross a very large sand barrier that definitely was a challenge for those who were not in good shape.

There was no vegetation whatsoever: no trees, no water fountain, no place to rest.

The South of France in the summer time is very hot. When the sun is high, at say 3pm, temperatures can reach 35°C or 40°C. Crossing this golden belt of sand was a considerable achievement.

In certain parts of The Sahara, the dunes were very high, and climbing them was strenuous. On their other side they were often formed into deep precipices and I accidentally rolled down into these a few times. It was frightening to be alone in these parts because I feared getting lost and being unable to get back to my parents' car.

As I walked along alone, the sand would burn my feet while at the same time I experienced the spiritual delights of peace and serenity. Then suddenly, from the top of a sandy ridge, the sea would appear like an endless blue carpet, sprinkled with foamy waves, repetitiously rolling and crashing with monotonous sounds on the shiny shore. For me, this was a paradise island.

This arid extremity of the peninsula was called "the beaches of L'Espiguette". Over the years, I've had many opportunities to catch glimpses of the "guardians" (modern-time cowboys) riding their white stallions on the beaches and driving ahead of them the wild horses known as "*les camarguais*". An unforgettable sight!

At the north end of the gulf, at what we called "the point of L'Espiguette", an impressive, gigantic lighthouse had been built after World War Two to warn the ships about the dangerous sandbanks. It had been designated a tourist attraction and few years earlier my parents and I had visited it together.

The Espiguette lighthouse was a massive, well designed and efficient edifice. It was manned around the clock, all year long, by a crew of professional guards.

The view from the top was breathtaking. The building did not have an elevator and we had to climb a narrow, winding staircase to reach the observatory area, just below the machine room.

The structure was about twenty-eight metres high. The lights were extraordinarily powerful, able to sweep the entire gulf as well as the two peninsulas, and thus help sailors not sure of the passage to see their way into harbour. As for the two smaller lighthouses at the harbour entrance, they served to warn boats about treacherous rocks and other hazardous obstacles, thus helping them to reach port safely. From the top of the lighthouse, I remember watching fishing boats pulling in their nets, swimmers, tourists water skiing or parasailing, the coastguard practicing safety drills, and even a French Navy submarine, in the docks for repairs. Occasionally, foreign tankers would pass far out at sea and blow their sirens. Many neighbouring resorts were visible on the horizon. These included the city of Montpellier, les Saintes-Maries de La Mer, Le Port de La Grande Motte-Carnon, Palavas les Flots, and the medieval town of Aigues-Mortes.

On the way to Le Grau du Roi, we had to pass through Nimes, a city with wonderful vestiges of Roman architecture, including an arena.

Further east we had to cross *La Camargue*, a large natural park of unparalleled untamed beauty. In this territory lived wild horses and protected bird species such as flamingos. There were large rice paddy-fields and corn-fields. As for human beings, for decades the Camargue had been the home of the "guardians". Living frugally, these ranchers bred large black bulls, small white stallions (*les camarguais*) and other horses with unique characteristics, sought after all around the world. In the 1960s, this very prosperous piece of land was already internationally renowned and providing France with resources like sea salt, rice, cattle, corn, fruit and vegetables. In addition, its vineyards proclaimed the merits of the top producers and the French government.

Our next stop before Le Grau du Roi was the historic village of Aigues-Mortes, a National Heritage site. Its medieval fortifications, original ramparts and authentic deep moats had experienced many expeditions at the time of the crusades. During the traditional pilgrimage seasons (May and October), visitors from the four corners of the globe came to attend religious services and ceremonies along the coast of the South of France.

To coincide with these, the town council had organized several very enjoyable activities, including competitive jousting, bull-fighting, rodeos and – similar to what is done in Pamplona – wild black bulls and horses were let loose inside the town walls.

The challenge was not to get caught (or hurt) by the animals running all over the streets and pavements.

These folkloric programmes had become so famous that the adjoining communities had created their own festivities and attractions.

From the observation deck of the lighthouse, these small thriving tourist centres and ports seemed to be links in a small chain along the coastline.

The magnificent structure of the lighthouse had become part of the local tradition and an official "must-see" for tourists.

But then, there was the "Ghost"!

CHAPTER FIFTEEN
THE SHRIEKING WHALE

People either believe or don't believe in ghosts, it's as simple as that. If castles, homes and museums can have their own spirits of the dead, why can't a lighthouse? So what was the story with L'Espiguette?

A nasty phantom had decided to haunt the building because of a whale – that's right! – because of a large blue whale, wounded and lost at sea, that came to die on the Mediterranean shore of the South of France in the early 1950s.

Blue whales usually live in the North Sea or other cold waters, and no one really knew why she had drifted so far away from home. There were a lot of bite marks on her, however. She had probably been hurt and then relentlessly attacked by sharks as she journeyed along. Finding her, the fishermen and other locals rushed to the site and believed that she had already died.

Mr Chauvin, a very prominent captain of the French Navy and owner of a few fishing boats in town, told everyone to start cutting into her to get her skin and grease. Her heart, brain and liver were also to be removed, saved and sold for a very high price.

Nobody was really concerned about saving the whale, and within a few hours, sailors and fishermen from the adjoining ports were all coming to get a piece of her. It was a free-for-all. The story goes that she was not dead but probably sleeping or resting. As soon as the people started to cut into her, shrieks could be heard miles away.

Nobody stopped.

Trawlers had brought harpoons to finish the killing. The animal was huge and it went on for hours. It was bloody and gory, her cries for help were almost human and her suffering must have been unimaginable.

Mr Chauvin had stayed in charge throughout the entire process. The shrill screams went on and on and it was late into the night when they eventually stopped.

The mammal's remains were left on the beach until fishing boats dragged her carcass out to sea and sank it to the bottom. The beach was cleaned up.

It was as though the incident never occurred. But I was curious to find out the details about this unspeakable atrocity.

There are always two sides to every story and in this case it wasn't any different.

Over the years, I had managed to speak with a few folk who had witnessed the gore and the long drawn-out suffering of the mammal. They confirmed the callousness of the culprits, who had totally lacked any consideration for her condition. But others swore that her death had been quick. Several fishermen even declared that she had probably died upon reaching the shore. They could not remember any shrieks or human-like screams made by the whale. They denied the killing.

However, Mr Chauvin, who was a prominent citizen and very powerful within the entire region, had undoubtedly guided the slaughter. He had given the directives to the locals and coerced them into butchering the whale.

All in all, I never found out the truth but I noticed a lot of reluctance from the populace in regard to answering questions about the incident. One thing for sure, the lighthouse was haunted by two spirits.

One was the whale, asserting her presence by means of piercing screams, loud breathing sounds and terrible wails, reminding everyone of her atrocious fate.

The other was Mr Chauvin's ghost.

Evidently, a few weeks after the trawlers had dumped the carcass at sea, a violent storm had struck the region and waves ten metres high came crushing into the harbour, flooding the beaches, hammering the moles and the lighthouses.

The wind blew ferociously, breaking windows, trees, and destroying everything in its path.

Swimmers caught in the storm were drowned and the coastguard was placed on high alert.

There were a few fishing boats still at sea fighting their way back to port, and their radio frequency was connected to the central switchboard of the regional navy rescue centre.

Retail stores, restaurants, and movie theatres were temporarily shut down for public safety. One of the trawlers in distress belonged to Mr Chauvin's fleet and he was on board that day, piloting the vessel himself.

Local authorities had total confidence that he and his crew would make it back home safely as he was an expert navigator, the weather forecast was fairly optimistic and the tempest blew out in a fury over Le Grau de Roi.

Somehow all the fishing boats came back with their crew alive and well, all but one, Mr Chauvin's.

Had it found refuge in another harbour? Had it sunk?

CHAPTER SIXTEEN
CAPTAIN CHAUVIN'S FATE

Obviously a lot of questions were raised about why Mr Chauvin's trawler had vanished. People in small towns and particularly in seaports are extremely superstitious; and tongues are loosened easily after a few glasses of wine.

I found out that, as soon as the weather had calmed, the municipality faced a much more dramatic turn of events. The entire area had suffered huge property damage and the number of victims was unfortunately high. Although not on the fishing vessels previously mentioned, some had drowned, a few had died of cuts from glass windows shattered by the violent winds, others had suffered heart attacks, and the rain had caused many car accidents and bad falls for those who were not able to take shelter fast enough when the gale's fury had reached its peak.

The natural elements had gone berserk and had struck the port with considerable force. However, the locals had a lot of willpower and went to work immediately to repair the damage and eventually rebuilt the town so it looked as though nothing had ever happened.

Meanwhile, the coastguard and the gendarmes were actively looking for Captain Chauvin's trawler and its crew. Finally, it was found drifting at large, a few nautical miles away from the peninsulas, and it was in bad shape.

The vessel had taken a serious beating, but because it was originally built as a lifeboat and had a specially constructed hull, it had not capsized. It had bounced like a cork amid the monstrous waves but never sank.

When the emergency patrol found it, the engines were flooded, the cabin on the deck was partially destroyed and the radio and electronic equipment were out of order. In addition, the rudder was broken.

A navy tow-ship brought it back to port where immediate medical attention was given to the survivors. Of the ten men on board six fishermen had been swept away by the raging waves including Captain Chauvin.

The gendarmes and the coastguard inspected the trawler inside-out for its compliance with safety regulations and to list major repairs to be undertaken.

On their hospital beds the four sailors told terrifying stories about what they had witnessed of their captain's death. The press got hold of them, and their testimonies were subsequently linked with the gruesome slaughter of the whale: immediately after this the lighthouse sightings began. These were the origins of the lighthouse ghosts.

I had been coming to Le Grau du Roi with my family for many years and heard all the tales and gossip associated with the area. The locals loved to talk but very often exaggerated.

In any case, L'Espiguette was supposedly possessed by evil spirits and the place had always fascinated me greatly.

During my week's holiday, I managed to meet one of the sailors who had survived the tempest and had worked on the "ghost trawler", as it came to be nicknamed by the inhabitants of Le Grau Roi.

The authorities had never found Mr Chauvin's body but the remains of two victims were thrown up by the waves, landing on the beach near the lighthouse. All in all, six brave fishermen including their captain had been victims of the deep. It was an act of God and if there was any consolation for this dramatic event, they had died doing what they loved most, being at sea.

I sat down with Etienne at a local bistro in front of a *café au lait et croissants*. He was a member of the crew who had confronted that formidable storm and had seen it all happen.

Etienne started to tell his story, and I listened. He narrated in a monotonous tone, moving his cigarette nervously between his fingers.

They were located south of the peninsulas when the weather started to turn for the worse. Very quickly, it became apparent to everyone on board that the storm which was approaching was of an unusual nature.

Captain Chauvin had been fishing for two days straight when he decided to return to port. The catch had been fruitful: the refrigerated compartments were full of sea bass, sardines, tuna, mackerel and more.

Etienne ordered another *café crème* and lit another cigarette, then he went on.

Other fishing boats were turning back and, like them also, they had been contacted by the navy search and rescue centre to stay on the same radio frequency, as a storm warning was in effect for the entire region.

All vessels were ordered to notify search and rescue once they were back in their port of call.

Etienne had faced thousands of squalls in his life. He had been a sailor since he was twelve years old.

He had witnessed much "crazy weather" as he said, but this was somehow different.

"How was it different, Etienne?" I asked.

"The speed with which all the natural elements combined was absolutely unprecedented," he answered.

He had tears in his eyes as he spoke. The violence of the wind, the incessant lightning and the sudden darkness made it very difficult to manœuvre even for an experienced pilot like Captain Chauvin.

Black clouds covered the sky, the temperature had dropped greatly within a mere half hour and the rain had turned to sleet.

The bridge and the deck were slippery. Thunder was rolling with deafening resonance. Lightning seemed to be aiming at the boat. It was wild! The waves were reaching ten to fifteen metres high. The wind was blowing with a force of 160 to 180 kilometres an hour. The air was frigid. Still Captain Chauvin did not panic!

"He was a true leader," Etienne stated.

"We were ordered to put on our safety jackets immediately and to stay at our posts no matter what," Etienne continued.

"From then on, strange events started to occur.

"Lightning hit us repeatedly setting fires at stern and starboard. It created some commotion but we extinguished them quickly.

"The boat was taking on water and we tried to start the pump without success.

"A very large wave crashed on the deck, breaking the mast. It fell on a crew member, Sylvio. He was badly hurt, screaming for help. As we tried to get to him, another wave rolled in and swept the wounded man and another sailor, Marcel, overboard.

"We were frantic and Captain Chauvin yelled at us to stay calm. We could not see our friends at all. They had been swallowed by the sea!

"We had now lost communication because the electronic equipment was wired into the mast.

"Our radio, CB radio and even the radar were destroyed. Water had penetrated the engine room.

"The motors were still working but we noticed that smoke was coming from below the deck and we heard huffs and puffs inside the engine room. These were not good signs at all.

"After a quick assessment of the damage, we had no choice but to try to stay alert and help the captain save the boat.

"The power of prayer is infinite in difficult moments. Everyone on board started to pray aloud. We definitely needed divine leadership. The crews were now scooping out water as best they could because the pumps did not work any more.

"It was all in vain. Finally the engines ceased and the vessel became like a cork floating on the top of the waves.

"Lightning struck us again, one at the bow and the other aft of the boat. The damage was more serious this time and the flames were hard to suppress.

"Luckily, the waves took care of it but the fire had destroyed our life boat and fishing gear.

"We were facing a catastrophe and there was not much we could do until the squall stopped altogether."

Etienne pursued his description of the events almost in a whisper. "Captain Chauvin had realized that we were all in grave danger but unfortunately he could not send a Mayday (*"venez m'aider"*) signal because the communication equipment had been rendered useless.

"He tried the beacon which was plugged into an electrical battery inside his cabin and luckily it worked.

"He emitted four or five SOS signals, hoping that the coastguards would see them.

"They did, but they were far too cautious to come out to save us, that's what is written in the official reports," said Etienne.

"All the other boats had returned to port, we were the only one still at large. The helicopters from the gendarmerie would not fly during the storm for safety reasons and nobody else had found us yet.

"We were bouncing up and down in the waves like on a roller coaster. We were constantly scooping out water from the boat and we had secured everything loose on the deck."

Etienne stopped for a few seconds and, from the terrace of the café where we sat, sadly looked at the sea on the horizon. The burning sun was high in the blue azure sky.

He continued, "Then we lost another good man. He was very experienced and one of the most accomplished fisherman around. The hatch of the engine-room had been left open and he was kneeling trying to get the motors started again. They were totally flooded, as large waves and brutal lightning were pounding us. It was a lost cause, but we had to try somehow, because without any mechanical power, we were prey to the tempest. He was a skilled technician and if someone could save us, it was him!

"On one side of the trapdoor two sailors were working in a frenzy to clear away as much water as possible, while he was repairing the fuel lines and putting new dry spark plugs on the diesels. It was hell in those conditions.

"Suddenly, a colossal purple flash crashed onto the deck and penetrated the inside of the vessel through the bow where the doors of the refrigerated compartments were situated. They had been secured but were still not completely tight. Lightning must find its way out and unfortunately it did so through the machine room. A high-pitched scream followed. We saw the sailor holding his hands to his face, and blood pouring through his fingers. He was in terrible pain, swaying from side to side in a state of shock."

Etienne told me that he had rushed to comfort him and give him first aid but the man was blinded, frantic and going all over the place. Then he fell overboard. In a split second Etienne managed to grab his right sleeve. He tried to hold onto him as long as he could, but he was not able to pull him back on deck.

The uncontrollable rocking of the boat, the nagging sleet and the force of the wind were too much for Etienne who could not lift the sailor's weight all by himself. He yelled for help and one man crawled towards him on the deck, which was as slippery as a skating-rink. Unexpectedly, the sleeve tore off and the sea swallowed the lightning-struck man in seconds. He did not have a chance.

Etienne was crying when he told me that he had looked into his friend's eyes but they were gone. It was horrifying. The motors had exploded in his face when they were hit by the lightning and he had been disfigured instantly.

Etienne added that strong gas fumes and sulphuric vapour enveloped the deck after the accident and Captain Chauvin was concerned about more fires arising on board because of the electric energy floating in the air. "We had now lost three men and the storm was still battling with full force," said Etienne.

I offered to take him for a walk along the moles so that he could relax, enjoy some fresh air and be able to finish his story which had captivated me. I was impressed with Etienne's memory of these dramatic events which had taken place ten or more years ago. He remembered all the relevant details.

Four sailors had come back alive from this dreadful disaster but Etienne was the only survivor who had agreed to recount his experiences.

I was told that the three other seamen who had been rescued did not wish to talk to anyone about the tragedy; in fact, they had refused to be interviewed on their hospital beds, ten years ago, right after the storm.

Eventually, they spoke to the gendarmes and other authorities in order to cooperate and help with the investigation of the deaths of their mates.

After the bodies of two brave sailors were found on shore, an official funeral ceremony took place in memory of all the victims of the squall.

Le Grau du Roi was in mourning. More than fifteen victims had been buried and close to another twenty persons had been seriously injured. It was a tremendous loss for such a small town. Nevertheless, life went on as usual, people got over it and dealt very well with their sorrow.

Etienne and I sat on the pier to talk some more. He pursued his story.

"The wind was howling, the sky had turned from black to grey and driving sleet continued to fall incessantly. The captain told us that the break in the sky could mean a change in the weather within a few hours. This was not really great consolation, but it gave us some courage at the time. He had manned the wheel all along and looked exhausted. We were all exhausted.

"Once again we prayed for our missing friends and asked the Lord to keep us alive so that we could have the opportunity to see our families again. We all wanted to get back home safely.

"Captain Chauvin wanted to ditch the trawler on a sandbank near the lighthouse of L'Espiguette. But without engines or communication systems, and three crew members short, it was an impossible task."

I noticed that Etienne was still disturbed by the tragedy. He came close to my face and articulated a little louder: "Gerard, we always believed that the devil was on the boat that night."

"When the main mast came down with brute force on the deck and crushed Sylvio's legs, it was so heavy that we would never have been able to lift it up using our physical force alone, but the waves were so high and mighty, so impetuous and fierce that they carried Sylvio and Marcel, the main mast and the heavy nets attached to it, as easily as if they were matchsticks, engulfing everything in seconds."

Etienne had never witnessed such destruction or intense fury from the elements in his entire maritime career.

Standing on the moles, he pointed out the area where the trawler had been shaken like an empty shell by the colossal waves.

"Sylvio and Marcel were good friends and expert seamen, I still think of them everyday," Etienne sighed.

"The succession of disasters progressed too quickly, the weather changed twice within a few hours and went from bad to worse without any warning. In retrospect the way my friends died was too horrible to accept and should never have occurred on this fishing-boat. Six very experienced sailors – including a very skillful navy captain – died on that expedition during a freak storm. This is unheard of.

"Gerard, I still shiver thinking of that journey. Philippe lost his face in the incident, he suffered a gruesome death and frankly speaking," he added, "it was better for him to rest with the Lord than to have survived and remain disfigured for life.

"I know for sure that Satan was all around us. If you had an opportunity to speak with the other survivors they would have told you the same thing. We all saw the devil and heard him too," said Etienne.

CHAPTER SEVENTEEN
TRAWLER POSSESSED

Do you think that the vessel was cursed?" I asked Etienne.

"As fishermen we all know the risks that we incur by being at sea every day. I have witnessed very strange events and some were actually inexplicable. I have fought many tempests throughout my career and even went overboard twice and was rescued. However, this particular storm and the loss of my six friends were the work of supernatural powers. It was a demoniac manifestation.

"It was revenge!

"At the end of my story, you will finally understand why."

"Please Etienne, tell me the rest of the story, let's sit down for a while," I begged.

So he went on. "The boat was rocking all over the place, the waves were ten to fifteen metres high, the captain used the fog-horn several times to alert and signal our position to any rescuer within the area. Apart from the beacon, it was the only apparatus left working on the boat at the time. But no one came to save us.

"Suddenly, a large pall of black smoke moved in, high above us. It was not cloud, it was dense and odourless, more like a huge thick cloak rolling out very rapidly over the sky. I felt very uneasy. I had never observed such a phenomenon before. None of us knew what it was. The forces of the wind and the waves' proportions diminished almost instantly. We were now rolling in five to seven-metre high swells. There was no strong current and the sleet had ceased completely. A very light rain was falling and the cold air had been replaced by a breeze.

"We were looking at each other, speechless and even the captain who had sailed all over the world did not know what to make of it. He shrugged his shoulders and we all hoped for the best. The sea was still turbulent and with the black sky over us the water looked grey and sombre. The trawler was still shaking back and forth, rolling sideways. We noticed a change in the force of the storm, it had drastically reduced.

"We all felt some reassurance and thought that perhaps it was all going to end soon."

Etienne's hands were trembling as he pulled out a cigarette. "That's when the devil took over," he said to me.

I kept silent and he continued the saga.

"The sky's colour was not natural. It appeared thick and inky and it made no reflections whatsoever in the sea. We all felt the presence of a black shadow, hovering over us.

"Observing the changes in the weather, Captain Chauvin seemed very intrigued. He too sensed that something strange, sinister and dangerous had moved upon us and wrapped the vessel in a thick cloak.

"Unexpectedly, coming from nowhere, we heard a long howl, so powerful that it reverberated all around us; it was followed by chuckling sounds and boisterous laughter.

"'What was that?' we asked the captain.

"'I don't know, men, but we are tired, stressed out; the most important thing right now is to remain calm. Let's not pay attention to the sounds, it could be the wind playing tricks on us,' he replied.

"We then concentrated on the boat, cleaning up the deck, scooping out water from the engine room and tightening any loose equipment which had been knocked around by the wind.

"Still, we all knew very well what we had heard! Gerard, it was Lucifer himself!" exclaimed Etienne.

This time I chose not to interrupt Etienne, so he could move on with the story.

"The water had calmed down, the rain was pouring gently and a light breeze was blowing. We all asked ourselves if the tempest was over once and for all.

"But the devil had not finished his destructive and wicked deeds, the trawler was doomed, no matter what!" shouted Etienne.

"The captain felt uneasy about the whole thing and had told us to stay alert because the weather could turn around at any time. It was very dark and the thick black sky made us nervous.

"Julien was the quartermaster and, on a fishing boat, his duties were diverse. The waves had receded and he went aft to check on the rudder's condition and the pulley which had possibly been damaged.

"The temperature was not freezing anymore but it was still chilly, although humid. The vessel was still rocking up and down pretty hard. Julien was holding on to one of the poles at the stern, trying, in precarious conditions, to complete his inspection. He had one leg inside the boat and the other resting on the small platform on the outside of the stern.

"Normally, to perform this task, Julien would dive into the water and take a look under the hull, swimming back and forth along the trawler, but not on a stormy day."

Etienne pondered for a while and carried on with the story: "Julien was standing on the platform at the stern because he had noticed that something was wrong with the equipment.

"Another sailor, Pierrot, and I went to help him.

"The fishing nets had become entangled in the rudder and the propeller, and we could not roll them back on the net drums because the motor operating the pulley had been flooded during the squall.

"We attempted to lift them up by hand but it was impossible without getting into the water and the sea was still too rough to permit it.

"The captain had asked us to safeguard the nets as he had been worried that the pressure and jolts created by the violent waves could unlatch the tumbler and send it to the bottom.

"Julien was kneeling on the platform, pulling hard. We were trying to be careful with the propeller's blades, but frankly speaking it was very difficult to work under those conditions.

"Then the demon decided to take Julien away!" shouted Etienne.

"Coming from nowhere, a large wave smashed into the vessel, and everything went haywire for us all over again!

"The boat jerked, rocked, moved up and down and tilted sideways dangerously; we were hopeless prisoners of the waters, bouncing about in a wooden shell. The sea looked grey and foamy," said Etienne. "Furthermore we had become the prey of Satan."

"Very strong vibrations were felt on the deck, we had to grab and hold onto anything we could, so as not to be thrown overboard. Some of the younger crew were frantic and the captain had to calm them.

"The trawler was undeniably possessed," said Etienne, nodding his head. "At that point, the wheel started spinning out of control, it went round and round at full speed and the captain had to let it go.

"The vessel was now in the Devil's hands."

"Julien was holding onto the poles with both hands and had not been able to step back inside the boat. We tried with might and main to pull him back in but he would not let go of the poles.

"We begged him to grab our arms and hands but he did not react. He seemed terrified, he had glassy eyes and he was holding the bars so tightly that his knuckles were white.

"I had never seen him so scared before, never! Something or someone had spooked him to death!

"He was obviously in shock, stiff. He kept screaming out, 'Please help me, help, not him again, not him!'"

"Who was he referring to?" I asked Etienne.

He replied, "I don't know. Julien was a true sailor, tough, courageous and the captain trusted him fully as the second-in-command. Yes, we had just braved a hell of a storm but we all handled it well. It had been testing for sure, nevertheless we were all experienced and up to that point Julien had never let us down, showing a lot of courage. Sylvio, Marcel and Philippe had lost their lives, but this type of work bears risks, we all knew what they were. The captain and Julien gave us the necessary leadership to carry on, we trusted them and they counted on us as well.

"We were all professionals; now, however, all had changed somehow. I did not understand what Julien was saying, Gerard. None of us did. I repeat that he had seen someone or something hellish and that he was in a state of panic.

"The captain came closer and spoke with Julien. He reasoned with him, offering a helping hand, asking him questions to keep his mind in motion.

"Nothing worked. The captain tried reassuring him.

"'Please,' he said to Julien, 'Grab my hand! Step inside! I need you and we all want to know what has troubled you this way. We also need your help, Julien. What has scared you? We need to know. Look, the sea is still rough, the weather is really bizarre and you might fall overboard. We need you, you're my second-in-command. Please Julien, pull yourself together, step back inside!'

"The captain was trying hard, but Julien did not reply.

"He only kept mumbling: 'Help me, he wants me, not him, not me please!'

"We were standing at the stern facing him in a semicircle, when a bursting, sardonic laugh erupted from the sky!

"It was loud and scary and it confused us all.

"At the same time, the net slowly rose from the sea, like a snake, and in a flash twirled around Julien's neck.

"It held him above the water for a few seconds, so all of us could watch the ensuing drowning.

"We were all shocked and petrified. It was horrific!

"The fishing net had freed itself from the equipment under the trawler and had become alive, it was a long snake, an enemy, and it was attacking us," cried Etienne.

"Julien was being strangled and then he was pulled under the water.

"It was so dark that we could see nothing.

"We all looked around the boat. Nothing. The net was unrolling from the drums. – The squeaky noise was driving us crazy! – Then it stopped.

"With a gigantic splash, Julien was hurled out of the water, the net tight around his neck and it held him out in the air, hanging like a rag doll!

"Gerard, it was mocking us, challenging us, this thing was killing Julien and we were impotent, we could not save him!

"He was still alive at that moment, his lips were moving a little, the net was standing straight up, balancing his body like a pendulum, then it plunged under one more time.

"There was total silence, then just the sound of the water crashing against the hull of boat.

"The captain was repeating 'My God, My God, what is happening to us?'

"A few very long minutes passed.

"In the few minutes that followed, we heard a long whistling sound followed by raucous laughter spreading across the black sky.

"Satan was mocking us Gerard, he was challenging us! How we hated him!

"Shooting straight out of the water, Julien's body emerged. He was now entirely wrapped up inside the net from head to toe. He was not moving, his skin had become wax-like, his eyes were closed, and his hands which were hanging at the sides of his body were clenched tight.

"The diabolic mesh which was holding Julien four to five metres above water then demonstrated its superiority by executing him in front of us."

"What happened next, Etienne?" I whispered.

Etienne wiped the tears from his face and replied,   "It broke his neck! Keeping his body in the air; it started to squeeze Julien's neck tighter and tighter until it snapped.

"We all heard the horrible cracking sound before the head tilted forward.

"The monster had won. At that precise moment the sky resounded with laughter, insulting and deriding us," Etienne cried out.

"The 'serpent net' shook its prey violently, so as to keep our attention focused, and then plunged into the grey waters for ever.

"It was the last time we saw Julien," sobbed Etienne.

"We all searched around the trawler for a few minutes but he was not to be seen.

"The captain said: 'It's over, men!'

"At that instant, the fishing net – which was at that point still attached to the net drums – broke free.

"It separated from the pulley as if it had been cut by a razor blade. We all looked at each other in dismay. The young apprentices recently hired as crew-members were sitting on the deck crying, holding on to each other.

"They were still teenagers and understandably frightened.

"We comforted them the best way we could, under the circumstances.

"Gerard, we were all scared, trust me; even the captain. But we could not show it to the rookies. If we did, the leadership on the vessel would collapse and that would mean grave danger when at sea.

"The captain, who had just lost his second mate, turned toward me and announced: 'Etienne, you are now the quartermaster!' I did not know what to reply.

"Normally, Gerard, I would have jumped for joy, because receiving such a promotion from Captain Chauvin meant that you really deserved it.

"He was a hard man to please. He was very sparse with compliments and favours, including promotions. I know that I thanked him nevertheless, and he shook my hand. Once again we all started to clean up the mess on the deck, scrutinizing the horizon for ships or helicopters which surely by now would have been sent out by the search and rescue teams.

"It was strange that we had not seen anybody and I had an uncanny feeling that we could not be found for a reason.

"The inky sky and grey waters felt like a malignant pall covering us, as if we were selectively lost on purpose.

"Yes, I had this nauseating sensation in my guts. I did confer with the captain about it. He looked at me and answered: 'Yes, I know, but please do not tell the others, try to motivate them instead!'

"Gerard, I was now very concerned about our salvation but we had to keep busy and hoped for the best," said Etienne.

"We kept busy on deck while the engine room was dried by two young sailors.

"Suddenly, a powerful thrust pushed the boat forward and the rocking, tilting and bouncing started all over again.

"I remembered yelling 'Now stop! Who are you? What do you want from us? No more!'"

"Looking at the sea which was relatively calm, this manifestation was clearly intentional and mischievous, instigated by the devil himself.

"For a few minutes we were vigorously shaken before a thick bluish mist formed around us accompanied by a rumbling noise, it sounded somewhat like turbines and we all felt trepidations on deck.

"We were watching the sea and tightly holding poles and handles throughout this episode.

"'Look at those lights!' the captain yelled while pointing starboard.

"Yes, huge green fluorescent lights were moving about under the hull. Circular in shape, they seemed to dance around the vessel and their reverberations illuminated the grey waters.

"'What are those?' we inquired.

"'I have no idea,' replied the captain.

"We moved slowly around the trawler, trying to find out what these bright green illuminations were all about.

"They flickered, changed direction, appeared and disappeared at intervals. It was very strange.

"A strident, shrill sound pierced the air and the entire boat began to levitate, rising at least three metres above the water as if lifted by invisible hands.

"A diabolic laugh erupted before we were dropped back into the sea like a stone.

"Luckily the vessel was very strong and was not damaged.

"Where did that extraordinary force come from?" Etienne hissed as he continued his tale. "These inexplicable demonstrations of power had only one purpose: To break our spirits and souls, nothing else!"

We were now walking back from the moles taking a leisurely route and crossing a sandy beach along the largest peninsula. I knew that he still had more of the story to tell, and I wanted to hear it all.

"Following the latest occurrences, a heavy silence settled among the crew," stated Etienne.

"We could not comprehend what had taken place earlier and we wished that it had just been a bad dream.

"But frankly speaking, we had witnessed something extraordinary which was not only unique but real and scary.

"Strangely, we had stopped spinning aimlessly out of control and the captain resumed command of his vessel; however, without engines and radio we could only pray for a search and rescue patrol to find us.

"We were perplexed and nervous and asked ourselves several times: *Will we ever be found? Is the devil playing with us?* Personally, I had this gut feeling that we had been purposely isolated from the original storm and that we had been transported into a twilight zone, but I did not know exactly why or how," explained Etienne.

"Some of the crew had tried unsuccessfully to repair the radio and the engines, but the damage was too extensive, beyond repair. Using the beacon, we all took turns to send SOS messages again.

"We were still drifting in grey waters under a thick inky sky but there were no more screams, no more laughter in the air, and the green lights had vanished from underneath and around the vessel. They were all gone but for how long?

"We were not sure of anything anymore. At every moment, we anticipated the worst!"

CHAPTER EIGHTEEN
A STRANGER ON BOARD

Another victim of this tragedy was a fisherman called Pierrot, and Etienne now began to talk about him. "He was a very strong man, extremely agile and blessed with a good sense of humour. His parents came from the Azores and were fishermen from generations past. The sea was in his blood and he was the best sailor around. Actually, over the years, many competitors tried to lure him away, but Pierrot enjoyed working with us, and for Captain Chauvin. He loved fishing. I sincerely believe that it was not work for him but simply a passion. He was always in a good mood, laughing and telling jokes. His life focused around the sea and football. He watched any and all football games whenever he found time. He himself was a gifted football player. Pierrot's trademark was to walk barefoot. He never wore sandals on board boat nor in the streets either. I don't think that he ever owned a pair of shoes," said Etienne. "He actually played football barefoot with the local team," he added.

"What happened to him?" I inquired.

"The devil killed him too," Etienne answered sadly.

"So Pierrot was victim number five?" I asked.

"Yes, and the captain was the last one to die," Etienne whispered.

Etienne and I sat on a big rock looking at the blue sea. From where we were, we could distinguish the 'Espiguette' lighthouse amid the sandy dunes. Even though it was very far away, its shape was clearly identifiable.

"Please tell me the end of the story, Etienne," I begged him.

And so he did.

"We were all waiting anxiously to find out what would be coming at us next," he continued. "It did not take long to happen. The green lights reappeared below the surface of the water, flashing on and off, circling around the boat, and a roaring sound followed them.

"Very quickly it increased in volume until it became too much to bear for us. We covered our ears, but in vain.

"The vessel started spinning around uncontrollably, faster and faster. It was totally out of the captain's control, and we could hear him swearing inside his cabin.

"And then the thing came out of the water until it was hovering above us."

"What thing, Etienne?" I eagerly inquired.

"A UFO, *une soucoupe volante*, a flying-saucer, Gerard," he replied.

"It was black in colour, not shiny but dull, it had lights all around it, coloured lights, it was circular in shape and we could not see any windows or portholes.

"It was very big, maybe ten metres in diameter.

"It was unbelievable! Can you imagine it, Gerard? And we were not drunk! What I am telling you is all true! We were paralyzed, afraid; it was like we were watching a movie! We had just gone through one of the craziest storms ever. We had lost friends at sea and then a UFO came at us out of the Mediterranean!

"The alien machine had steam coming out from underneath it; it generated various sounds and stayed idling above us for a long time.

"There was so much power coming out of its vents that we felt crushed and could not move.

"It was perhaps five metres above us, no more.

"There was a very bright illumination all around the UFO and we could not look at it directly for anything but a very short time.

"I can't remember any more particular details. Only what I have just told you."

"Then what happened, Etienne? Please continue!" I insisted.

"That's when everything went crazy. A strident sound came out of the machine, and everything on deck went flying! Buckets, poles, mops, equipment, tool boxes, all were thrown around. The windows of the captain's cabin exploded and we all ducked for safety.

"That's when the harpoon killed Pierrot," Etienne said.

"How did it happen?" I asked.

"The harpoon must have been left on deck earlier, when we had tried to untie Julien from the fishing-net. Pierrot was holding onto the empty window-frame of the captain's cabin, standing up near the cabin door. As I told you, the windows had been shattered by the sound coming out of the machine's turbines. Pierrot was yelling something at the captain. We could not hear what he was saying.

"Suddenly, all was quiet. The UFO was still floating over us, but there was now a humming noise in the air. We all looked at each other, we were not talking.

"Pierrot was still standing at the same spot by the captain's cabin. We then saw the harpoon rise up slowly from the stern area. It moved into a horizontal position, parallel to the deck, then it stood still menacingly, its hook and dart facing Pierrot.

"We did not even have the opportunity to warn him. Its speed was like lightning. It flew with so much power that the hook and its dart went through Pierrot's throat and then through the captain's cabin door.

"Pierrot did not have a chance, he died instantly. We tried to free him but did not succeed. The harpoon had pierced the wooden door and the the wall behind it with such force that it was impossible to get it loose.

"We just left Pierrot dangling there helplessly. Only Satan can perform such horrible deeds!" said Etienne with tears in his eyes.

I stayed silent and dared not interrupt him. He continued: "We had all watched Pierrot's death in horror and we saw the captain cry for the first time.

"Then the UFO began to take some more altitude. It was still above us, making the same humming sound.

"At the same time, we were instructed by the captain to stay alert, not move but try to remember as many details as possible of what was taking place. He insisted that the authorities would want to know what had happened to us and our lost friends.

"We all agreed, but frankly speaking, Gerard, I did not think that any of us remaining on board would come out of the experience alive. It did not look good at all!

"We heard two popping sounds and right out of the water emerged two fluorescent spheres. Both were made of a shiny type of metal, resembling silver. The two spheres were surrounded by coloured halos, blue, purple, green, and red. They flew close to the spacecraft and placed themselves immediately underneath it.

"The colours intensified and became brighter. Both silver balls started moving rapidly back and forth.

"We watched this event without saying a word.

"Meanwhile the sky cleared completely. The clouds, the black ink pall, the rain, the sleet, the wind, all disappeared in a matter of minutes. Blue azure patches, showing rays of sun, started forming above us. Was it too good to be true?

"'Now what?' we all thought.

"Even the sea around us began to look blue again. Was it finally over?

"The remaining clouds dissipated quickly and we could see to the northeast, on the horizon, the Espiguette lighthouse.

"So we now realised, as a matter of fact, that we had never been too far away from the shore or from the peninsula.

"We were surprised, but now felt much safer. The captain told us that help should not be too long in arriving, particularly with the weather clearing up.

"Then without warning, the two little spheres sped away from the spacecraft towards the shoreline. They were so fast that our eyes could not possibly follow their trajectories; the speed was incredible. They did not even make a sound, just zoomed through the air.

"A few minutes later, the flying-saucer rose up to a height of about sixty metres and vanished in front of our eyes.

"To tell you the truth, we were all happy to see these strange machines go away!

"The weather was improving by the minute and the captain was looking out for rescue boats while we were peered at the sky for planes or helicopters, since the gendarmes would surely be looking for us."

Etienne stopped for a minute to light up a cigarette. He did not say a word. He put the cigarette out after a few puffs.

"The captain, Etienne, what happened?"

"Captain Chauvin was scanning the sea with his binoculars, hoping to find and secure help. He moved aft, port, starboard, stern, and finally went back to the bow.

"He then climbed on a large tool box to get a better view and I remember that he was muttering under his breath to himself; meanwhile, I asked the three rookies to see to the deck. These boys were having a difficult time coping with all the tragedies. It was important to keep them busy and motivated.

"Captain Chauvin wanted the boat to look clean and organized even though we had faced so much hardship. He always said that a vessel's appearance reflected on its captain's style of leadership.

"The sky continued to clear rapidly, the sun was shining and warming the air. We were hoping with all our hearts to get towed to port but we did not see any search and rescue boats. We all thought that this was very odd indeed.

"The young sailors were picking up debris, cleaning the deck, and I was helping the captain to send new SOS signals with the beacon.

"Somehow I suddenly had a strange feeling that we were being observed. I left the cabin and slowly walked around the deck.

"The captain asked me, 'What is it? What's wrong, Etienne?'

"'Captain, there is a stranger on board. I feel it. There is an ominous presence here,' I told him.

"'Come on, Etienne! Nonsense! It's only the five of us left on the boat here,' he replied.

"At that moment, a shapeless form, shadow-like, black like soot and very thin appeared at the bow of the vessel. It had come out of nowhere, without a sound.

"Within seconds it took on the semblance of a dark hooded robe and pointed a thin finger at the impaled body.

"We all watched this apparition in awe. We could not understand where it had come from or what it meant. Who was it? What did it want from us? Suddenly it turned around and we clearly noticed that the hood was empty, there was no face inside it; the robe was not carried by feet but was simply floating above the deck.

"The thin finger protruding from the right sleeve was now aiming at Captain Chauvin, who was looking straight at the empty hood without saying a single word.

"The captain kept his sang-froid throughout this scary encounter.

"From where I was positioned, I noticed that the faceless shadow had no left hand either, it was simply an empty habit with a devilish soul inside.

"Gerard, it was an odd and frightening episode," Etienne said, looking at me with pain in his eyes.

"For a few more seconds the ghost looked intensely at the captain and made a life-terminating gesture with its index finger before disintegrating in front of our eyes.

"A cloud of black ash flew overboard and dissolved above the waves."

"'What was that, Captain?' the rookies asked in unison.

"'It was a personal message from down below, to my attention only,' he replied stoically.

"What did it mean, Captain?" I insisted on asking him myself.

"But he never had time to answer my question because at that instant, a gigantic swordfish jumped out of the water and pierced the captain's chest with its long pointed sword!"

CHAPTER NINETEEN
THE DEVIL'S HELPER

In one motion the tail of the swordfish hit the deck, and using it as a trampoline, the enormous predator dived back into the blue water with its prey speared through and through.

"It happened so quickly that we had no time to react.

"We all rushed to the side of the boat to see if we could find the captain, but the fish had plunged with him and had not resurfaced.

"Swordfishes can reach depths of 900 metres," Etienne said. "We all knew that the captain was certainly dead but we wanted to secure his body and take it back with us.

"'There, look, it's him!' the rookies yelled.

"And there it was, the swordfish: jumping, diving, jumping higher, and diving again, with its victim still dangling on its sword.

"This time, the fish was mocking us, provoking us, but what could we do? Nothing, just watch and be enraged.

"It was the largest swordfish that I've ever seen," said Etienne. "I've caught thousands in my life, but this one was a monster!"

"How big was it?" I inquired.

"At least five metres and 600 kilos," answered Etienne.

"But this beast enjoyed killing. It specifically targeted the captain and took pleasure in drowning him and taunting us by playing with his body.

"And moreover, Gerard, this swordfish had supernatural powers, it was the devil's helper."

"Why do you say that?" I asked.

"Our fishing boat was the largest around, and this monster could leap into the air and over our boat, carrying a dead man's weight effortlessly on its nose, and it did the same thing a few times in a matter of minutes. That is why," he replied.

"Another thing, fishes have cold eyes; this one did not. It had human eyes, they were expressive. It enjoyed killing. The last bounce over the stern was unbelievable. It jumped at least ten metres into the air, then it screamed and its eyes were red like hot iron, angry, demonic. It plunged into the water, went under the hull, emerging at the bow, then sprang up into the air ten metres high above the surface again. Then it screamed for joy and vanished into the blue sea forever."

"Etienne, you mentioned screams, what screams?" I asked.

"That's another thing, swordfishes don't scream at sea: whales and dolphins do. They even talk. They make sounds above and underwater. But swordfish do not.

"This one did, every time it dived or jumped we could hear it, a heinous high-pitched laugh. It was very strange, again almost human.

"Do you really believe that this predator was an accomplice of evil? It was a big fish, Etienne, that's all!"

"No, I will always maintain that it was sent to execute the captain. The jumps, the eyes, the laughs, and when it touched the water, the sea bubbled around its body like it was on fire. Yes, Gerard, this beast was sent by Satan!

"It could easily have impaled me or the rookies. We were all there. But it especially chose our leader. Remember the black robe? The captain knew that he would die next, a curse was put upon him and the swordfish performed the duty. What a gruesome death, Gerard, to be killed by a swordfish and drowned under your own boat! I will never forget that fishing trip!

"Do you want to know something bizarre?" continued Etienne.

"Please tell me," I answered.

"Captain Chauvin's trawler was called *L'Espadon* – *The Swordfish*," he replied with a sardonic smile on his face.

This time my mouth opened, but I remained speechless!

All I can say is that it was ironic, to say the least. Could it possibly have been more than coincidence? Was it perhaps fate? These were questions for which no one could have answers.

Etienne and I took another walk as he was progressing through this extraordinary story.

"I was now leading a marooned vessel with three very frightened rookies as my mates. We began scrutinizing the horizon again to search for rescue."

"'Etienne, look, at the lighthouse!' shouted one of the rookies.

"A colossal ball of fire – there's no other way to describe it – was rolling above the water in the area of the Espiguette lighthouse.

"Earlier, the UFOs had flown in that direction; undoubtedly, this new sighting was associated with them.

"We all watched the huge ball rocking with the waves for a while until, without warning, it abruptly shot off into the sky and disappeared.

"There was no noise, no explosion, just an immense illumination, free of any heat rays. It was gone as fast as it had appeared and with such speed that we could not follow it with the naked eye.

"Strangely enough the gendarmes later found foreigners on the beaches of L'Espiguette," said Etienne.

"Foreigners? What foreigners?" I inquired.

"Nobody had seen the ball of light or the UFOs. But later on, some tourists called the gendarmes because they had come across cattle and domestic animals wandering along the beach."

"What kind of animals, Etienne?"

"Cows, sheep, goats, roosters, even emus."

"Who were the strangers, Etienne?"

"People who spoke some form of Chinese language. It was later established that these families were from Western China and Tibet. They did not possess any identification papers and had no passports."

Above all, they did not remember having landed there.

I was listening attentively to this strange event and somehow associated Eudoxus with it all.

"It must have made the news everywhere, Etienne," I suggested.

"Not at all! – City Hall buried it."

"You see, even though it was an amazing occurrence, it could have had negative consequences for Le Grau du Roi. The mayor categorically refused to discuss the matter; it was all hushed up, there was no media report.

"The foreigners were sent back home, all expenses paid. As for the animals, they were taken to some farms near Montpellier."

"Have you ever gone back to sea, Etienne, since this horrifying fishing trip?" I asked.

"Yes. It happened more than ten years ago, you know. Time heals everything in the long run. Even so, I will never be the same again.

"The rookies are now fishermen and they all have good jobs on large trawlers. It was difficult for them at first, but they all conquered their fears and followed my advice, which was to make sure that they went back to work right away, and they did," said Etienne.

We walked along the pier in silence and came back to the town. We sat at the terrace of a local bistro and ordered lunch and two pastis liqueurs.

I wanted to know the end of the adventure.

"How did you get rescued, Etienne? How did they find you?"

"The storm had completely cleared, the sea was now calm and our position was not precarious. I had a very good intuition that we would be found within a few hours.

"Meanwhile, we tidied up the boat, as it was a real mess.

"That's when one of the rookies found a wooden box which had been stashed below deck.

"It contained two flares and an alarm pistol, the type used to send a distress signal."

"Why didn't the captain use it earlier?" I inquired.

"I don't know, Gerard, unless he believed that the weather was too stormy for a rescue and that he ought to wait for a more opportune time to use it. However, I never understood why these flares were not kept in his cabin," he added. "That's where they should have been in the first place. It was still daylight, but we sent off one flare anyway, and kept one for night time, just in case.

"We also covered Pierrot's body with blankets as a mark of respect and common decency. And then we waited. About two hours later, a helicopter from the gendarmerie flew over the ship; we yelled and sent the second flare into the air. They saw us.

"Very soon we were surrounded by the coastguard, the local rescue ships and the Navy patrol boats.

"*L'Espadon* was towed away into the port of Le Grau du Roi, where it was thoroughly searched and examined.

"The rookies and I were eventually interrogated at great length. Police detectives investigated the disappearance of our friends and fellow crew-members, the death of Captain Chauvin, and of course Pierrot's death also. Six persons missing at once!

"The rescue officers and the local gendarmerie asked us all kinds of questions over and over again. There was finally an official inquest and some publicity ensued.

"Throughout all this our reports coincided with each other. They seemed of course far-fetched for the investigators and the court, but we stuck to our stories, after all they were true!

"Sylvio and Marcel's bodies had been found on the beaches of L'Espiguette, the town had sustained loss of life and damage to property because of the storm, and *L'Espadon* was the substantial evidence of it all.

"Not to forget that domestic animals were found astray on beaches and that Chinese people without any identification papers or passports were also found there. Gerard, the local authorities had a lot on their hands!"

"Were any doubts expressed about your or the rookies' integrity throughout the proceedings?" I inquired.

"Not really. Each of us had a good reputation and we did not try to hide anything of what we had seen, even if it sounded unbelievable at times.

"The gendarmes asked us a lot of particulars about the UFO sightings, which we of course provided to the best of our abilities. However, City Hall and the mayor himself wanted a quick end to it all.

"*L'Espadon*'s misfortune was starting to create gossip and controversial rumours, which might have been very damaging for Le Grau du Roi, as they might have turned into inflammatory press reviews and negative publicity.

"The investigation was closed rapidly, followed by a short announcement to the media. It was concluded that Le Grau du Roi had been hit by a colossal sea storm which was an act of God, and consequently *L'Espadon* had been the victim of a freak maritime accident.

"The six sailors who had died received posthumous awards for bravery.

"After the incident, I took a few weeks off to clear my head. Later I was hired as second-in-command on a large trawler and that is what I do to this day."

"And what happened to *L'Espadon*?" I asked.

"*L'Espadon* ultimately was fully repaired and bought by a fishing company from Palavas. It still sails today in its entire splendour. Fishermen are very superstitious by nature and nobody around here wanted to have anything to do with it."

"Etienne, what do you think about the stories regarding the Espiguette lighthouse? I mean Captain Chauvin's ghost and the whale crying. Do you believe in these? Frankly speaking, I have not seen or heard anything out of the ordinary at the lighthouse, whether during the day or at night, therefore I cannot comment."

"I believe in ghosts," he answered gravely.

CHAPTER TWENTY
ETIENNE'S STORY

We ordered two more espressos and continued to talk. I had used my own powers of deduction to reach a sensible conclusion with regard to this exceptional story, but I wanted to hear Etienne's.

He had had more than ten years to ponder the episode.

He began with the lighthouse ghost stories. He insisted that they were not to be connected in any way with the events which took place on *L'Espadon*.

The revenge of the whale and Captain Chauvin's curse were simply folktales following the trawler's recovery, which had leaked to the press by means of unauthorized and sensitive disclosures made at the inquest. Etienne brushed them aside, calling them absurd and without foundation.

He also told me that his narrative had opened old wounds, and that grief still haunts him to this day causing him sorrow and bringing back memories of his lost mates; however, he realized and accepted that life must go on, no matter what.

When he went back to sea employed on another trawler, he had to shake off the fears and inner demons that were harassing him. By helping the rookies do the same, he regained his self confidence, comfort and peace of mind.

Then he brought up the topic of the unexplained UFOs and their controversial manifestation at L'Espiguette.

"Pure coincidence. No more, no less," stated Etienne. "The flying-saucer was already on site and was going to emerge sooner or later. The storm did not precipitate anything.

"Nonetheless, I am glad that I witnessed it. I was a sceptic, but now I even believe that aliens live among us and that their landing at L'Espiguette was indisputable proof of this."

He spoke again about the gigantic storm, saying he was certain that it was an act of God. He felt very sad about the large death toll and the many injured, but this was predetermined, he felt.

"The Lord had made his decision," he maintained.

"What about the other unusual happenings, Etienne?"

"I am a religious man, Gerard; and at my age, I can assure you that luck means nothing. It does not even exist, only fate exists.

"On that terrible day, *L'Espadon* was to be the site of a struggle between our Lord and Satan. If I escaped death along with the rookies it's because God had made that decision; it was our destiny.

"On that voyage, my guardian angel was protecting me, so I survived the ordeal and so did the rookies. The Lord, the angels, and Lucifer are always near us, and their powers control everything that happens in our lives.

"They are our doom and destiny combined in fact. The devil used some of his diabolical tricks to kill my mates and the captain. He even isolated us in a thick, black cloud to perform his deeds. The black robes, the swordfish, the possessed fishing net were all Satan's weapons.

"There was no divine intervention throughout the battle on the part of the Lord. Satan took away my mates, but in the end Jesus saved me and the rookies," said Etienne.

I could see that he had made his peace with it all. He had been a very interesting raconteur but it was now time to part. I thanked him and shook his hand profusely. As I crossed the bridge to return to my hotel, we waved goodbye to each other.

I felt somehow very privileged because Etienne's revelations about the horrific fishing trip had never been made public by the investigators, but he had confided in me its most specific details from beginning to end.

I had heard the most fascinating story in my life disclosed by someone who had lived it first hand.

Later that afternoon, I drove to L'Espiguette with my family.

From the top of the lighthouse, I contemplated The Sahara and its golden dunes, the blue sea, the foaming waves crashing on the never-ending beaches covered with sand.

I did not see any ghosts, nor did I hear any whales shrieking, and I never came face to face with an angry Captain Chauvin. It was simply a lighthouse overlooking Le Grau du Roi and its peninsulas.

Driving back to Aix-en-Provence in my parents' car, I was debating whether or not ghosts really existed. On the one hand, Etienne felt that the local tales about the Espiguette lighthouse were fictitious; nevertheless, he gave unconditional credence to the existence of ghosts.

Furthermore, parts of my mind were concentrating on the circumstances of Etienne's frightful fishing trip while others were considering the involvement of Eudoxus with the UFO manifestation during the storm. Some questions were nagging me. Why was the spacecraft under water? Was the storm created as a form of experiment or was it a true act of God? Why did Chinese citizens and domestic animals appear on these particular beaches? – I could not answer any of these questions but still they wouldn't leave my head.

It would be almost another year before Eudoxus appeared in my life, again in very dramatic circumstances.

CHAPTER TWENTY-ONE
A WISE DECISION

I was working extremely long hours during my apprenticeship at Le Vendôme.

Shifts were often scheduled back to back and I would come home exhausted around 2am, but had to be ready to start again at 8am sharp the next day with very little sleep.

Wages were low, the schedules merciless, but I still enjoyed the job because I was acquiring a tremendous amount of knowledge and expertise.

I lived some two kilometres away from the job. I traveled the distance on foot because there was no bus service late at night.

Later on, I bought a Velosolex, an inexpensive and economical mode of transportation, very popular in France.

I enjoyed jogging or running late during the spring; it cleared my head after a hard day's work and it was good physical exercise.

On one particular day the weather was superb, it must have been around 1am, and I clearly remember the full moon illuminating the sky, surrounded by a multitude of bright tiny stars.

It was very quiet and peaceful. There was absolutely no traffic along La Route de Marseilles, the main highway connecting Aix-en-Provence to Marseilles, the second largest city in France.

I was marching along at a good pace and I had reached the corner of a famous local hospital.

Well, I've done a quarter of the way, I told myself.

Suddenly I heard the roaring of an engine approaching very quickly. I recognized a sports car driving in my direction, I even heard the sound of the gears shifting. It was moving at a very high speed.

I hope that this car can make the bend, I thought to myself. There was a very sharp curve just at the junction of the hospital and it had been the site of many accidents over the years.

But the driver went through it very quickly without any difficulties. He was at the wheel of an MG, a small two-seater British car.

The noise of the motor resonated like thunder through the serene night, the automobile zoomed down the highway and as it passed me I noticed its dark green colour and the distinctive spoked wheels with the MG emblem in the centre.

Suddenly, about two hundred metres down the road, it pulled up at the curb with its emergency lights flashing.

The driver honked the horn a few times to attract my attention, so I began to run to find out if he needed my help. When I reached the vehicle he inquired where I was going and if I needed a lift.

I politely replied that I lived nearby and that I did not need a ride home.

The man was in his late twenties and spoke in broken French with an American accent.

He opened the passenger door and asked me to get in, I could smell liquor on his breath and hesitated.

"Please, jump in, have no fear, it will save you some time, it's too late to walk home," he insisted.

At that moment I heard a loud voice in the air telling me, "No, don't get in! walk away!"

I froze and looked up across the road. In the green bushes surmounting the sidewalk a tall human form was standing like a statue. I could not distinguish all the details but it was a man, thin, tall in stature, very pale and he was enveloped in a greenish halo. It gave him a very unusual aura.

"Walk away, don't join him!" the voice resonated through the air.

I was transfixed, staring at that strange ghost-like figure across the highway and I did not move.

"Who is that?" I thought.

"Come on, I don't have all night, are you coming or not?" yelled the man angrily.

His jacket and tie were undone and he was wearing leather racing gloves, he was getting very impatient.

"No thank you, sir, I'll keep walking home. I only have twenty more minutes to go. Thank you for your offer, though," I replied politely.

The American muttered something, probably profanities, slammed the passenger door shut and drove away like mad, spinning his tyres.

I stood there motionless and as I looked across the road there was nothing unusual there at all, just green bushes, trees and spring flowers lining the pavement. There was nobody standing on the small grass hill.

Who did I see? Who had warned me not to ride with the stranger? And why?

I was soon to find out the reason.

I started jogging again and I could still hear the car barrelling down La Route de Marseilles, the driver was shifting gears rapidly. The clatter of the muffler was ear-splitting even from a distance.

He's going too fast, I said to myself. I increased my pace.

A few minutes passed and then a loud bang resounded, followed in quick succession by the squeaking of tyres, the spinning of an engine, metallic clangs and finally a small explosion. Then total silence.

I knew that a terrible accident had happened and that the American driver had probably missed the bend at Le Pont de L'Arc. It was an overpass above the Arc River, forming an extension of the highway in a very dangerous curve.

It had claimed many victims over the years, including a bus full of children which had missed the turn and plunged thirty-five metres below into the river; no one had survived the fall.

Immediately I sprinted to the scene of the collision.

While approaching the area, I could hear sirens in the background. The ambulance or the firemen are on the way, I thought to myself.

When I arrived at the scene the ambulance was already there. It was complete mayhem; it had been a very ugly accident.

The car had skidded at the curve, hit an electric pole, spun around and struck the bridge's protective ramp. There were tyre-marks all over the highway and the bend. The vehicle was a total write-off. Its hood and hub caps had gone flying. Two of the wheels had landed on the side of the pavement and the headlights had been smashed.

The driver was still in his seat and he was not moving; his face was covered in blood because his head had gone through the windscreen.

The ambulance attendant checked the driver closely, and in one motion pulled him out of the car by his belt and under his arms. He placed the American on a stretcher.

"How is he?" I asked quietly.

"Dead! He's dead, son!" he replied.

There was a strong smell of gasoline, and I noticed that the car's tank was leaking profusely.

"You'd better leave, son. We turned off the ignition but you never know, the car could still catch fire," the attendant said.

A few minutes later, the gendarmes and the fire trucks arrived at the same time. The car and the road were sprayed abundantly to prevent any risk of fire or explosion, the traffic being re-routed during this clean-up.

I walked away, thinking that if I had accepted that stranger's proposition, I would have been killed with him. But who had saved me? Again this thought was profoundly troubling.

Was it Eudoxus himself or one of his aides? Could it have been his extreme powers of persuasion or even intuition reaching me at the right time? Or did I experience a true divine intervention? The Lord works in mysterious ways and if it is not our time we do not go, no matter what.

I reached my home, happy but deeply confused. I had no answers to these questions and was unable to understand what had happened to me earlier.

I had escaped a deadly road accident, not because of physical circumstances, but due to a spiritual interference.

Whichever way I looked at it, it had worked in my favour; it was not luck but fate again!

For years since then I have been intrigued by the mysterious apparition which saved my life. I have never found out who – or what – protected me, but I do know that I narrowly escaped death. It has been difficult to forget this episode because some of its elements were so tragic. I have always been thankful that it had a safe outcome for myself.

They say that time helps you forget, but not in this case. I still remember each detail of that warm spring night, like it was yesterday. I know with certainty that I had a vision. Someone gave me a sign, a life-saving call from beyond. Deep in my heart, I feel that it was Eudoxus who saved me.

CHAPTER TWENTY-TWO
FROM HOTEL TO BOOT CAMP

My training at Le Vendôme restaurant in Aix-en-Provence had ended. I went to gain additional experience by working at two exclusive winter resorts located in the French Alps, one in Chamonix, the other in Vars les Claux. Then because I had always dreamt of seeing the French Riviera, I wrote an application letter to a hotel that was then more select than the most select in France, the Hôtel de Paris in Monte Carlo.

To this day, it is still one of the best hotels in the world. They accepted me and I spent two years at this establishment, first one full year prior to my military service and then for a full year after I was demobilized.

It was one of the best jobs in my life. The working conditions were excellent and it gave me the unique opportunity to meet the rich and famous of the 1960s: Aristotle Onassis and Maria Callas, Prince Rainier of Monaco and Grace Kelly, the Beatles, the Rolling Stones, David Niven, Jackie Stewart, Brigitte Bardot, Katherine Hepburn, Steve McQueen, Roger Moore, Barbara Hutton and many many more.

Day after day I gazed in awe at the glitter and wealth of this little principality and its glamorous and luxurious casino.

At the hotel they taught me how to give faultless service, how to handle critical situations with tact, intelligence, class and above all discretion. I was truly inspired by the staff's professionalism and dedication.

This magnificent institution laid the final foundation stone for my future career, placing a cap on my apprenticeship. It was a valuable teaching ground, and the hotel's letter of reference was worth any college diploma.

Soon I received my conscription card and left for Moselle in the eastern part of France, an area where the sky is grey and the winters are horribly cold.

I was based on the German border at the largest military camp in France, close to the old Maginot Line of World War Two. I was nineteen years old.

It was going to be hard, challenging and definitely unforgettable. But you know, I enjoyed my military life.

As a soldier you never forget the moments of joy, sorrow or gloom that you share with your buddies, the pains and hardship of training, the sweat, the bitter cold and the scorching heat that you endure during military manœuvres. Above all you never forget the unbreakable bonds and camaraderie that hold a team together.

I went through two months of boot camp, followed by driving school and two weeks of jump school in the Southwest of France at ETAP (*Ecole des Troupes Aéroportées*, School of Airborne Troops) in Pau.

Being a member of a combat company also meant daily routines of marksmanship, obstacle courses and long marches.

We never stayed put at the camp for long; we were always on training or on a mission somewhere else.

In the spring, a few of us were selected for jungle warfare so we went to French Guyana for four weeks, to join a French foreign legion regiment which taught us how to survive and fight in this hostile environment.

It was the hardest thing that I have ever done in my lifetime.

We all lost so much weight that our uniforms did not fit us any longer. But we had only been back to base for two weeks when our new order came through. We were leaving for a very special course, four weeks in duration, at the commando training centre of Mont Louis in the Pyrenees. The objective was to obtain the coveted French commando training badge, the CNEC (Centre National d'Entrainement Commando) badge.

Upon our arrival, the colonel in charge told us that he was going to transform our bodies and minds and show us how to become professional soldiers. And you know what? He did. Once I wore that badge, I was never the same person again.

CHAPTER TWENTY-THREE
THE FAULTY TANK

Eudoxus saved my life again during my military service. The incident took place amidst an international exercise in Germany, combining with foreign forces.

We were based for a month in Immendingen, Germany at the home of the Third Parachute Hussar Regiment (RHP, *Régiment de Hussards Parachutistes*). It was November and snow had already started to fall, it was very cold.

We were demonstrating to the high brass how to place a mine under a moving vehicle such as a tank, jeep, truck, bus or any other similar target.

We took turns exhibiting our skills.

There were French, German, British, American, Italian, and Australian officers watching us and making notes.

We were supposed to run to the side of a tank or a Light Armoured Vehicle (VBL, *Véhicule Blindé Léger*), roll into a pit and stick the mine on to and underneath the vehicle when it passed over our head. Then we were to exit at the other end and run back to our original position. My turn came up and I started running alongside an AMX-10RC Wheeled Recon Vehicle and Tank Destroyer, I overtook it, I saw the hole and rolled into it.

I waited for the tank to arrive.

It did not, I heard it very close but it had stopped.

I waited. I wondered what had happened; then its engine made a strange noise like it was choking.

It moved forward and I could see the long barrel of its gun above my head, but I could not come out because my orders were to place the mine underneath the AMX and that's what I was going to do.

The vehicle's tracks were advancing, slowly covering the hole; then the engine died altogether. There was total silence, something was definitely wrong.

The pit started to crumble around me, it had been dug quickly and it was not very deep, the sides were holding only because the ground froze soon after the digging and it was now covered in snow.

Tons of heavy metal were putting pressure on it; without any doubt it was going to collapse and I was going to be buried alive. I was in big trouble but kept very calm. I screamed and yelled but all in vain.

I was waist-deep in mud and wet snow; the armoured vehicle was not moving.

I was convinced that the pilots knew I was there and that they had radioed for help. The top brass who were watching the exercise must also have realized that something had gone wrong.

Help is on the way, I told myself.

Then, as dirt began to fall on my face, I began to pray aloud. I also begged Eudoxus to intervene and help me: "Please use your powers quickly or I'll die!"

A few seconds later, I heard the sound of a turbine loud and clear and I recognized it immediately; it was a spacecraft.

There was formidable suction above the hole where I was standing. I watched the tank being lifted up and disappear. Mud was flying everywhere and I could feel intense heat all over my body.

When I saw the blue sky I did not hesitate a second, I jumped out.

About ten metres away on my left stood the tank with its astonished personnel scratching their heads.

When they saw me they shook my hand vehemently, and apologized profusely because they knew that I had been trapped underneath. They had been terribly concerned but the vehicle had experienced a complete breakdown, involving also poor radio transmission. They had been waiting for help, which still had not arrived. They still could not understand how the AMX had leapt up ten metres away from the pit.

I suggested to the crew that we should complete the exercise as planned, because the officers and members of our company were watching us.

The tank started without a problem, I found another hole, rolled into it and placed the mine on the tank as instructed. All went well.

Upon my return to the starting point my Commanding Officer as well as other officers inquired about the incident that they had witnessed. I blamed mechanical failure for the delay. Obviously Eudoxus had made sure that no one could see the spacecraft!

The AMX was sent away for repairs and it was later confirmed that a faulty starter and electrical malfunction were the causes of the incident.

I thanked Eudoxus for saving my life once more, this time in full daylight!

Following the manœuvres in Germany, ten members of our company were sent to Chamonix, Mont Blanc, to the Military Mountain Training Centre (CEM) there. We stayed for three weeks climbing rocks, abseiling down cliffs, and practising mountain rescues.

It was awesome but extremely hard and perilous. We were taught by instructors of the National Rescue Team, who are specialized mountaineers, and by the Gendarmerie Rescue Team. These men were at the top of their fields and saved lives day after day in the most treacherous conditions. They were true heroes.

Once the course at Chamonix Mont Blanc ended, we returned to base in Moselle and were allowed to go on leave.

My military service was almost complete, and I planned to go back to the Hôtel de Paris in Monte Carlo for the summer season. I wanted to move to England in the autumn to learn English. I had acquired excellent references and I would have no difficulty in getting a work permit.

To stay in the army was no longer an option for me. I felt that I was not a military man at heart. The fact that I wanted to see the world and travel extensively meant that going back into the hospitality industry was the right choice to make.

During my demobilization period I had a lot of time to think about Eudoxus and how he had saved Valia's life and mine. I owed him a lot and wondered if we would ever meet again in the future.

Actually he was going to save my neck some time later in very hazardous circumstances.

Meanwhile I gazed everyday at the azure sky and sunbathed on the beaches in Monte Carlo. It was a wonderful change of scenery from the shivering cold of the Moselle, and I loved it!

While in Monaco, I patronized a bar which was known to be a recruiting centre for mercenaries. Once in a while men were interviewed in the bar basement for soldier of fortune duties and were signed up for missions around the world.

The African continent was always in turmoil and in those days foreigners were also enlisting to go to the Vietnam War.

More often than not it was not all about money, but also adventure. Individual units included former soldiers, officers, and sometimes civilian experts in their fields.

Former French legionnaires, Britons, Australians, Americans and South Africans made up the core of these mercenary units.

For centuries such men had used their skills all over the world; in the 1960s they fought rebel armies, protected expatriates and foreign nationals from ruthless tribes and even helped whoever was elected at the time to organize a government. Sometimes they would go the other way and set up a coup d'état to remove a dictator from power. They also guarded diamond mines or international oil fields. It was very common in Africa to have mercenaries escort a deposed leader or dictator to a safe haven after a coup d'état.

To this day, they are still very active and often hired as bodyguards and private security personnel.

At the café, I met a man called Georges, a former French Legionnaire during the Algerian war. He liked to reminisce about his military life and so did I. He also was a former paratrooper and had seen much action in North Africa. We became friends.

One day, he asked me point blank if I wanted to go to the Congo for an upcoming mission. Of course my answer was, "No way, I'm not cut out to be a mercenary."

My reasons were many. I had a personal friend in Aix-en-Provence who had gone to Africa on a mission and had returned with only his shirt on his back and no money in his pocket. Luckily for him he had not been wounded or killed. It had been a very harrowing experience for him. He expected adventure and financial reward. He received neither.

There was a risk of not getting paid at all. I was not ready to go for a thrill. Mercenaries were often caught in shabby deals and they had no recourse to receive their pay.

The chances of getting killed were high. They often did not obtain all the equipment requested and had to manage with what was given to them. Loss of life in covert operations was extensive.

There was no glory in these contracts, mercenaries fought for money, not medals like in the military. There was no honour. I did not like the idea at all.

Finally, corruption was rampant throughout most of the African states. No one could be trusted. The kings, prime ministers and presidents of these countries hired mercenaries for totally self-centered reasons.

Soldiers of fortune were often helping to overthrow a régime or back up a new dictatorship; their salaries were paid either in foreign currencies (US dollars or British pounds), or in diamonds, silver, or gold. It was risky and awkward.

When Georges asked me for the second time to join a mission in the Congo, I once again explained my reasons for not wanting to join. He listened attentively, but still wanted to brief me about the political status of the state.

Guerrilla warfare, political unrest and tribal fighting had been constantly looming across the nation since its 1960 independence from France. Heads of state changed up to three or four times a year, revolts and coups d'état took place routinely; the country had no government *per se*, it was in complete chaos. The Congo's political and economic instability were dangerous for its neighbouring African countries. Colonel Joseph Desire Mobutu was a tyrant in power, and the Katanga rebels were fighting the government fiercely. Lumumba had been assassinated in 1961 and this had left a gloomy feeling of anger and hopelessness across the country and throughout the world.

For a short time Moise Tshombe governed as the elected Prime Minister of the Congo. But soon the autocrat, Colonel Joseph-Désiré Mobutu came back to full power. He was always surrounded by mercenaries, and in some instances he called upon French troops to get him out of trouble with the rebels.

Georges wanted to show me a documentary, filmed by the French Foreign Legion around the city of Stanleyville. It was horrible, depicting massacres committed by three groups, Mobutu's own soldiers, Katanga rebels, and the crazy Simba warriors – "Simba" is the Swahili word for lions – who did not really support any political party but loved to kill and so took advantage of the wars taking place in the provinces.

The Simbas were ruthless, took drugs, were continually drunk, and practiced cannibalism openly. Their witch doctors always followed them in combat, they never fought at night or in the rain, and ate the heart and liver of their victims when still alive, so the documentary said.

They were feared by all. In this part of the world armed soldiers left their tanks, trucks, and jeeps, and ran away when the Simbas were coming to a city or village. All this flashed in front of my eyes while watching Georges' film.

It seemed to me that there was absolutely no chance of survival in the Congo. United Nations soldiers had been victims of snipers. Red Cross staff members and French troops had been ambushed and impaled. Foreign tourists were shot in their cars. Locals were hacked to death in their villages. French missionaries had been burnt alive with rubber tyres around their necks. It went on and on. Murders, atrocities, lootings, merciless killings. I kept silent and did not know what to say.

Then Georges asked me once more if I wanted to become a member of his team to fly to Stanleyville to extract 1500 civilians to safety in military aircraft, the points of return being Nice on the French Riviera and if necessary Paris as well.

The expatriates were professionals and their families, embassy workers, missionaries, French officials, teachers, and volunteers. If they were not evacuated at once, they would without any doubt, be killed, Georges said.

The operation would last a maximum of five days. We had to work in collaboration with the French Foreign Legion and two regiments of French paratroopers. It was definitely not a peace-keeping mission. Many of us were going to die. I had only four hours to decide if I was going to be a member of the team.

CHAPTER TWENTY-FOUR
IN THE CONGO

I needed some time to think about Georges' proposal. Why would I even consider risking my life by walking into such carnage? After all, it was not my country, it was not patriotism, it was not my business. But then those images from the documentary flashed in front of my eyes again and I saw the killings, the mutilations, the local civilians massacred, the white farmers being shot to death, and the terror of the expatriates. I felt sick to my stomach. I was also angry and all of a sudden I had the impulse to take action to help the foreigners.

Later I called Georges and we sat down together in the café basement. I decided to accept the challenge. He told me the details of the operation and paid me in advance half of my wages for the five days' job.

We left Nice airport the following day in a military C-160 AIR TRANSALL for Stanleyville, the capital of the Congo. We were a group of twenty men, eighteen French and two Britons. We were all silent on the flight. When we landed at Stanleyville, the heat was almost unbearable, and the stench was horrible. Machine-gun fire could be heard close by and the rebels were firing mortars right into the city streets. Mobutu's private guards and French paratroopers were protecting the airport, which was crucial for us because it was our only escape route. The Foreign Legion working with French security services had already accumulated a lot of reconnaissance information and had prepared lists of foreigners to be evacuated. Our job was to gather them together and put them safely on the planes as fast as possible.

Upon our arrival in the capital, we had a meeting with Georges who was our leader. We received uniforms, arms, ammunition, and discussed the logistics of the extraction.

We were introduced to officers of the French Legion. Then we were split into teams. To transport the refugees, we were given a military bus and two trucks with armed personnel on board.

To take the foreigners back home, Transall planes provided by the French government had been flying back and forth twice a day between Stanleyville and Paris or Nice. Georges informed us, however, that we would work around the clock because we had been ordered by the French Intelligence Service to complete the operation in three days rather than five.

The Simbas were everywhere in high numbers and had destroyed many villages, butchering men, women, and children. They were now targeting French soldiers, and it was becoming extremely dangerous.

Because they did not fight at night we could use that time to carry on our mission without much risk. We were ready.

My team of five left in a bus and drove through the city, picking up local civilians and Westerners. The Congolese did not want to leave. They loved their country but they had no safe place to go to. We were told to take them to a refugee camp set up by the Red Cross, close to the airport. They needed to be protected because the Katanga rebels and Simbas were waiting to kill them for no valid reason at all.

The Foreign Legion had also arranged helicopters to transport them to Cameroon, The Gabon or Angola, but it was taking time to be organized.

The first day was rough. We were pelted with cans, stones and bottles. The rebels shot at us but no one was injured.

We managed to take one hundred and fifty people to the airport in three different trips. The Transalls followed their schedules and flew five hundred civilians, including the one hundred and fifty we had gathered together, back to France. It went very well.

On the second day of the mission we received additional help. The United Nations (UN) troops provided armoured vehicles at the airport and jeeps to follow our teams around the villages.

The army officers were concerned about the condition of the tarmac and that was one of the reasons why they wanted to speed up the operation.

The second day was also difficult due to the fact that some white farmers did not want to leave their properties, but the UN forces finally persuaded them to do so and then they came with us.

The Simbas were closing in on the centre of Stanleyville. Fierce fighting took place with some minimal loss to the French troops.

On the second day, I made a big mistake.

German, Swedish, British, Belgian, and French embassy employees were to be evacuated at once. On the bus, we received a radio call to change direction in order to pick them up at a downtown hotel, where they were waiting for us.

We collected them safely and the bus was now full of foreigners. Some had children and all were frightened, but they were on their way out of Congo, alive and safe. They were certainly grateful for that.

I felt that I was doing something worthwhile. The Simbas were moving fast and they surely wanted to get to the airport; but the French troops and our team were pushing them back until the extraction was complete.

It was the most strategic area to be protected in order to accomplish our mission successfully.

We took back roads to our destination because the highway to the airport was too exposed to mortar fire. Suddenly we saw a car with two young white foreigners inside. It was a young German couple and it was certainly not the place to spend their honeymoon. They were surrounded by five Simba warriors, who were dancing around the car, screaming. The tourists were petrified.

One Simba aimed his gun at the man and shot him dead through the windshield. Another broke the side window and dragged the woman out of the car by the hair.

I stopped the bus and jumped out with my gun drawn. The driver shouted after me, "Stop, come back, don't go close to them!"

My partners followed me and I saw two foreign legionnaires from the truck behind us doing the same. We fired in unison at the Simbas, and a few seconds later they were lying dead on the ground.

The woman was sobbing uncontrollably, hysterical. I took her to the bus and soon the evacuees were boarding the Transall for Nice.

Georges had found two old planes in good condition to speed up the evacuation. Two mercenaries had pilot licenses and were going to fly the old Dakotas. We were on schedule and it looked as if we were going to finish the mission in three days as planned. With the embassy staff and families, the number of foreigners waiting to be evacuated out of the Congo now exceeded 1800, but with the two extra planes it did not present a major problem.

Our deadline had been set at 6pm on the third day. The Katanga rebels and Simbas were everywhere. There was such a large number of warriors, that we knew that our troops would not be able to hold them off much longer.

A few solders had been killed and the wounded were evacuated in the Transalls.

At the end of the second day, six flights had been successfully carried out and more than 1200 people had been evacuated to safety.

On the last day, we were expecting to rescue at least six hundred more men, women, and children, both locals and foreigners. We were looking at a very favourable outcome for our mission.

However, we had suffered a large number of casualties. Georges had been informed that a few more of our men and some more UN soldiers had been killed and a group of French paratroopers had been critically wounded near the airport.

This bad news did not help his mood and he gave me hell for jumping off the bus to save the German woman from the Simbas.

"Who do you think you are?" he yelled. "You jeopardized not only the mission but risked everyone else's life. Our escorts could have been killed needlessly. You were unprofessional! The mission, Gerard! Just follow my orders! The mission's all that counts! You acted on impulse, grow up!"

He walked away and I felt very bad. He was right and I apologized to him.

The third day was action day and Georges had already organized the teams, planes, and flight plans for the final evacuation trips to the Paris and Nice airports. We all woke up very early for the briefing. There had been very important phone calls from the Elysée Palace. Mobutu was in the hot seat with the French president who wanted assurances that all embassy employees would be brought back home safely and he also expected minimal losses to our troops. It meant that our mission had made big news, it was no longer a secret, and the world media were ready for wide coverage.

The expatriates were free to speak with the press but Georges advised us not to say anything to anyone upon our return to France. My orders were to patrol the small towns and villages around Stanleyville, check all the huts and bring foreigners and families to the base camp. I was provided with a list of names, which included engineers, nuns, doctors, nurses, teachers, missionaries, and Jesuit priests who had previously refused to leave. This was their last chance. If they did not leave, their slaughter by the Simbas was imminent.

Many Catholic missions had already been burned to the ground and their occupants hacked to death. Hospitals and schools were regularly ransacked and the patients and little children tortured or decapitated by the Katanga rebels or the Simbas.

The volunteers had always been the hardest to convince to leave; but this time we were going to urge them to pack and come with us at once. We knew that the fanatical warriors were in the area killing at random and that we did not have the manpower to stop them.

We drove north of the city on dirt roads in armoured vehicles with two empty military buses, accompanied by army trucks full of foreign troops and French paratroopers as escorts.

The sun was hot and the stench of death filled the air. Mutilated corpses were lying everywhere and wild dogs, pigs, and rats were feeding on them in a frenzy. Crows were circling above us cawing loudly. It was an awful sight. We could hear gun battles in the background and villagers screaming at their attackers. The Simbas were in the area and closing in.

We approached a small village bordering a river. There was a pontoon with fishing boats attached to it. The French soldiers secured the perimeter while we talked to the leaders. Luck was on our side. Upon being notified by the UN troops of our arrival, Americans, Australians, Canadians, Swedes, and French people located in the area had all gathered in this village for quick evacuation. They had all agreed to come with us and that was a relief. We could move on.

Throughout the day, we managed to cover a very large area circling Stanleyville. We cleared three villages and four Christian missions, but many of the natives refused to come with us and chose instead to hide in the forests or elsewhere to escape the warriors.

We all prayed for them. The UN soldiers were already overwhelmed by the crisis and could no longer protect them. They could not take them to the various borders to seek refuge because it was not their duty. The fate of these people was written; their lives were doomed.

I had accounted for virtually all on my name list and the buses were full. I had not realized that so many foreign volunteers worked in Africa on a permanent basis, coming from all over the world and exhibiting motivation, talent, and bravery.

One man on my list was still missing. I inquired on the bus if anyone knew where he was. Time was of the essence.

He was a French Jesuit priest who had been living peacefully in Africa among the natives for the past twenty years and it was not going to be easy to persuade him to come with us. He had a fairly large congregation and was highly respected among the locals. They were going to miss him a great deal. But we had to pull him out before it was too late.

We stopped briefly to get the right directions to the village from among those we were evacuating and I took this opportunity also to talk to Captain Lefort, the Commanding Officer of the French paratroopers. It was decided that, to avoid any dilemma, we would extract him by force if necessary, because the Simbas would otherwise certainly assassinate him before dusk.

He was living alone as all the other volunteers in the area had gone back to their respective countries. At one point in time there had been eight expatriates, including a doctor, nurses, a dentist, an engineer, a schoolteacher and even a former French gendarme who performed security duties.

Even though we had not so far encountered any resistance or attack from the enemy, we knew that they were following us very closely, waiting for the first opportunity to kill us all.

We drove three miles up a hill and then saw the village down a valley. We had to be quick and return to base camp before 6pm.

It was very nicely set up with gardens, trees, and a lake with a tiny fishing boat attached to a pole. The hospital, the school, and the church were all standing side by side in very good condition. There was even a water-well on a nearby hill.

The Jesuit's name was Jean Marc Lapineau. He had built this community from scratch and was admired and respected by all. No one knew his age, only that he was an old man but still very strong, who gave communion to his parishioners every Sunday.

We did not waste any time with Father Lapineau regarding the purpose of our visit. He, of course, vehemently refused to go with us. At that point, Captain Lefort showed him a set of handcuffs. "Do you want to wear them or not!" he said, "Your choice." The priest understood and came with us without a struggle. When he boarded the bus everyone applauded and greeted him. He was a local hero and I sat beside him. Father Lapineau kept silent. He looked gloomy and was almost in tears. However, he knew that he had to escape this hellish nightmare and destruction if he wanted to stay alive.

It was our last trip and we did not want any catastrophe to occur, so Captain Lefort had called for heavy reinforcements. Two tanks from the UN were going to wait for us two miles down the road where the roads to two villages intersected. Two helicopters from the French Parachute Regiment were going to hover above us armed with rockets and heavy machine guns. He also arranged the transport and escort line-up for the return to base camp.

The two buses were placed in the middle, the French legionnaires' truck at the front and the paratroopers in the rear. There would be a space of 100 metres between the buses and the tanks would be on each side keeping the enemy at bay. All vehicles were to maintain a high level of speed and they were not to stop for anything whatsoever. These were our orders.

We drove back down the trail and saw the two UN tanks firing at convoys full of Simba warriors. The two helicopters were hovering overhead, cutting down waves of rebels coming out of the bushes. Meanwhile the frightened passengers on the bus were holding tightly onto each other; a lot of the women and children were crying.

Captain Lefort instructed one tank operator to move up to the front line to clear our path. The other was protecting our left side and the helicopters were taking care of our right. I felt reassured with this idea; above all we had additional fire power in case of an attack. I prayed with all my heart that we would all reach the airport safely.

We were facing a situation which was not uncommon in the Congo. The Simbas were ferocious warriors, driven by drugs, alcohol and the thirst for blood. There were many of them, more than ten thousand it was said, but possibly there were even more.

The Katanga rebels were deserters, lost souls, traitors, unemployed and many of them former Mobutu loyalists. They were more than six thousand or perhaps eight thousand in number. They had joined the Simbas because they were scared to death of them. They had no real cause, just hatred of Mobutu.

The country's present army consisted of a small number of poorly paid and untrained men who were very much afraid of the two groups of rebels. That is why Mobutu constantly called upon France and Belgium to help him out. His army was unable to defend itself and corrupt.

We were now in the midst of it all trying to get out alive.

We drove past rice paddies and corn fields scattered with dead corpses, past farm houses, huts, and shacks which had been set on fire, and past Simbas murdering anyone in sight. We saw looting, soldiers and rebels drinking, dancing, and killing for pleasure all at the same time.

I turned to look at Father Lapineau by my side and asked him how he felt. He did not answer me but looked at me with very deep blue eyes. I had seen those eyes before, they did not look at me, but through me, it was a very strange feeling.

"You're not a mercenary, you have never been one, but you are a good soldier and your heart is at the right place. Never change, stay who you are! You are a child of the light. He will be your friend for ever. You are going to be wounded soon, but you will not die. Do not worry, you will be alright and we shall all get home safely."

I was astonished and replied awkwardly, "What did you say, Father?"

"You heard me, son! Stay with the Lord. Jesus and your far away friend are protecting you. I have nothing else to add. Let me be now, please." Continuing to look at me, he said: "You should look after the passengers, they need you more than ever, please give them courage!" Then he turned around and looked out of the window silently.

What was that about? I thought to myself. A Jesuit priest meddling with my mind during a precarious military mission! It was not good at all. I needed all my senses to concentrate. Who was Father Lapineau? Why had he said what he said?

I got up from my seat and walked up and down the aisle, smiling and reassuring the passengers. I even asked some parents to sing songs and get the children to join in. It worked! During that time I tried to look brave and fearless.

We were doing well, moving at a good speed, our escort of tanks and helicopters protecting us on our way to safety. Then Georges radioed me, suddenly wanting to know our exact position. I told him.

"Soon you will see a group of huts with a flagpole in the centre," he said. "There is a Red Cross emblem on the top of one of the huts. Get the nurse out of there, quickly. One minute, that's all you have."

I felt a knot in my stomach. Simbas, rebels, and drunken soldiers were everywhere. And I had to extract an expatriate in the middle of it all?

"Are you sure she is still there, Georges?" I asked.

"What do you mean?"

"All I can see from the bus are dead bodies, Simbas, rebels, and army soldiers drunk out of their minds!"

There was silence on the radio.

"Georges are you there, do you copy?"

"Maybe you're right, but we must be sure, she has not been seen in days, and has not written to her family in months. The Red Cross wants confirmation. She should be there or she is already dead. Please check it out. Get a lot of back up. I am going to talk to Lefort right now, good luck!"

I picked up my shotgun, checked my handgun, and told the driver where to stop.

Soon we were at the place Georges had described. On the right I could see the huts and the Red Cross symbol. I jumped out, followed by paratroopers and legionnaires. The site had not been torched and ransacked yet, but the Simbas and rebels were going to do that very soon.

I ran as fast as I could towards the huts. Behind me I could hear gunfire, rockets, and the helicopters with their machine guns covering me all the way.

There was nothing to be found. I looked everywhere. I saw nothing but dead babies with their mothers, lying motionless. I moved to the Red Cross hut. Still nothing. No trace of the nurse. In my mind I assumed that she had been kidnapped, tortured, and killed. If not, where else could she be?

All of a sudden, two Simbas burst into the hut. One was waving a spear; the other a bow and arrow. The spear man said: "A Frenchman, kill him!" I shot them both point-blank and they fell to the ground.

An excruciating pain on my right side made me scream and fall to my knees. An arrow had penetrated my body under the ribcage, and to make matters worse, it had not exited. The suffering was immediately unbearable.

I lay on my back and felt blood coming up into my mouth. I moved onto my side to vomit. It was hot, so hot. I could hear noises of fighting outside and people shouting. I could hear mortar fire and the helicopters' machine guns sweeping the area with their deadly bullets. My mouth was very dry. Why is nobody coming to help me? I thought.

I was mumbling some words, "Medic! Doctor! Help!" But I could not scream, I was in too much pain and the words were trapped in my throat.

I wanted to drink some water but knew that with my wound it would be a big mistake, I knew that I was dying because my shirt was soaked in blood and I was spitting out very dark coloured fluid, which meant that my liver had been punctured. I thought, Why here? Why now? What a horrible place to die! I felt very hot, I touched my face and found I was perspiring profusely. – Fever, I had a high fever. The Simbas always dipped their arrows into urine and faeces, my blood had been poisoned! – I said out loud, "Please Jesus, let me die quickly, don't let the Simbas take me prisoner!"

I looked at the arrow sticking out of my side. The fever was making me wander. I screamed, shouted, called names, begged the Lord. But no one was listening. No sound was coming out of my mouth; just a lot of blood. I was in intolerable pain; it was like a burning fire inside my body.

Water, I needed water, I looked around without moving my torso but could not see any. How long would it be before I would die? Please Jesus, make it quick, my time has come, I thought. Why, Lord, do you prolong the agony?

Then I passed out; I do not know how long I was unconscious. My brain began to work in a strange and incomprehensible manner, sending me images and faces of people that I had known in the past. I even saw the passengers in the bus looking out of the windows in distress, and Father Lapineau smiling at me. Did it mean that I was already dead? Probably yes, because my life was passing in front of my eyes.

In my delirium, for a while I felt no more pain. I did not hear any battles, any gunfire, any screams, and my body was no longer aching.

But then, "Do not pull out the arrow, do not touch it!" I heard myself scream. It was pitch black, all around me. "It hurts so much, leave it inside. I am thirsty, please give me some water. Georges will be angry because I got wounded. I was stupid not to have moved fast enough. Now everyone will be killed because of me. Why am I blind? I can hear chirping noises, where are they coming from? Why can't I move? My shoulders are stuck to the ground. I feel hands touching me. Who is it? I can't see anything and these chirping noises are driving me crazy. Why do I feel so relaxed? I do not feel any pain, but I am so thirsty, please give me water. If I am already dead why are they touching me? Why?"

I heard more voices talking softly. The images kept rolling before my eyes. I saw primary school teachers, high school and soccer games, my army buddies, my brother, my parents, Georges in Monaco, my work, Eudoxus and the spacecraft, all moving in and out like a camera with its film rolling.

My mouth was dry, I wanted water. A tube slid between my lips, it tasted nice, fresh like a fruit juice, I knew this flavour. I'd had it before.

CHAPTER TWENTY-FIVE
EUDOXUS AND THE MATHESUS STONE

Someone was talking softly to me, his lips close to my ear. I recognized that voice. "Do not move Gerard," it said. "Do not say a word but look at me."

I opened my eyes and Eudoxus was there. He was on his knees working on my wound. With him were three little grey men with big black eyes running around the hut with surgical tools in their hands.

"Please drink more of that juice. It is a vitamin and it will clean up your blood. It was poisoned by the infected arrow but you will not need a transfusion. Your liver is fine, we cauterized it. It will heal very soon. The scar is very small and should disappear in a few days. All you need to do now is rest. You were very seriously injured."

"Eudoxus, how did you know? How did you come here?"

"Do not worry about that, you know that I will always be there for you in any serious emergency, and this was a matter of life and death, wasn't it?" he was smiling.

"Yes it was, Eudoxus," I whispered.

"Gerard, we must go now, you are fine. Please rest for a few days. When your officers question you, you do not recall anything, okay? Just listen to what they have to say, do not argue or make conversation with them. All you have to tell them," he added, "is that you were out cold after being injured, it's that simple."

"Yes, Eudoxus, I promise you that I will not discuss anything with anyone."

He nodded in approval. Then he handed me his belt. "Now, touch the Mathesus stone to heal your body completely. It's essential for your recovery."

I placed my right palm onto the reddish stone and almost immediately it began to sparkle and get redder and redder. A buzzing sound and streaks of coloured light filled the hut while strong vibrations shook my body. It was so powerful that I had difficulty holding the gem even with both hands. Eudoxus was watching. A surge of energy spread through me like a bolt of lightning. I felt pain no more, but my right side was itchy. I drank another glass of the sweet blue nectar. Eudoxus took the Mathesus stone out of his belt and placed it onto my wound. I screamed at the piercing burning sensation. Eudoxus explained that this was the final step in cauterizing my internal organs as well as the external lesion. I was finally healed.

I drank one more glass of the stimulant and Eudoxus massaged my head with the precious gem. It felt soothing and made me feel very relaxed. At the same time the little aliens kneaded my body from head to toe, making their usual chirping sounds.

Then Eudoxus placed the Mathesus stone on the top of my belly. After a minute or so, he nodded and fixed it back into his belt. I felt tired and drowsy.

I looked around the hut and it had not been disturbed. The bloodied arrow was lying on a surgical cloth by my side and the two dead Simbas were still lying on the floor. Eudoxus looked at me and said, "We have to leave now. You will be home soon. Of course we shall meet again in the future because I always keep my eye on you. You should rest now."

"Eudoxus," I replied, "there is a war outside. Nobody followed me into the hut to look for me. Why was that? What has happened?"

"Remember the time warp, Gerard! That's the reason! You will shortly be found by your officers and everything will become as usual. Do not worry!"

I sat up to say something to him, but he turned around, spoke briskly to his assistants, and then they all vanished through the walls of the hut like ghosts.

Eudoxus had amazed me once again. I stared at the wall, shaking my head in disbelief but with a smile on my face, thinking that they had walked through it like phantoms without leaving any trace.

I peered through the hut door but could not see anything because it was raining very hard, with lightning and thunder cracking loudly. I thought about my escorts, Lefort, and his men. Where had they all gone? I could not hear any gunfire, mortars, or helicopters hovering. It was very, very strange.

I looked outside again. The weather was horrid but even from this distance I could see the bus still sitting idle on the road. I knew that I had not gone mad and that I was not dreaming these events, because my shirt was stained with blood and two Simba warriors were lying dead at my feet. My brain was numb, I was tired, and just wanted to sleep. Because the hut was a small Red Cross hospital there was a pharmacy and a surgical table inside it. I lay down on it and fell asleep.

"Here he is! Medic, check him over quickly and we'll carry him to the bus on a stretcher!" Captain Lefort was in the hut giving orders to his men. "How do you feel, son? By the way, where did the doctor go?"

"I am fine, I can walk. What doctor, captain?"

"The tall blond American with his three nurses."

"I do not know, Captain, I was unconscious, I'm the only one here. And two dead Simbas," and I pointed them out to Lefort.

He looked at me strangely, glanced around the hut, and sent his men outside in search of the doctor.

The medic examined my wound and turned to Lefort, astonished. "Captain, you should see this, he only has a tiny scar on the right side. It's incredible!"

Lefort picked up the bloodied arrow and said to me: "This thing causes major damage. I believe the doctor mentioned that it had pierced your liver. It was a fatal injury. By now you should be with the angels, not walking around."

"I have never seen anything like it," said the medic.

Captain Lefort was shaking his head with a frown on his face and he asked me, "Can you walk to the bus? We should move quickly."

"Yes, no problem!" I stood up and we left the hut.

The patrol had returned empty-handed and there was no trace of the doctor and his nurses. They had simply vanished from the face of the Earth.

It was not raining so hard anymore but black clouds were still covering the sky, plunging the entire area into darkness.

Lefort escorted me to the bus and when I boarded everyone cheered. The passengers were clapping their hands, whistling and hugging me. It was a great feeling.

I was a little weak but I knew that I could handle the trip back home without any problem.

Lefort ordered the tanks back into position. He also asked the two helicopters to fly over us at low altitude and arranged for the UN forces to follow us to base camp.

I sat back beside Father Lapineau. He smiled at me, gave me a wink and said, "I told you, didn't I? Are you okay now?"

"Yes, I am, Father," I replied.

"Good. Take it easy. It's over. We are safe now. These people will never have any idea of what happened to you, you know. Your friend saved your life. It's your secret, do not divulge it." He turned away from me and looked out of the window.

What a strange person Father Lapineau was! Who was he really? I wondered.

The convoy was moving at a slower pace than before, because the road was muddy and there was a risk of the buses getting stuck. But the tank in front of us, with its heavy tracks, kept the trail as practicable as possible.

The severe rain and the darkness had forced the rebels and the Simbas back to their hideouts. When Lefort announced that the airport was safe and that the enemy had finally retreated, all the passengers were ecstatic with joy.

I eyed Father Lapineau, who was dozing on his seat, and my mind flew back to Eudoxus. His timing had been perfect. By frightening and overpowering the Simbas through rain, storm, and darkness, he had not only saved my life but had saved us all. I knew that it was Eudoxus who had created those critical distractions, and so did the secretive Father Lapineau.

Could Father Lapineau be an alien? Did he know Eudoxus? Was he really a Jesuit priest or an extra terrestrial sent to Earth as an observer? Obviously these were questions I could not answer, they were mere suppositions. In fact, I preferred not to know the answers. Eudoxus had told me once that some secrets are better left unexplained; that's why they were secrets.

At that moment Georges radioed Lefort that more government employees were waiting to be transported to the airport. Due to the political unrest and random killings, more countries had closed their embassies for safety reasons. So we now had to fly their employees to France and from there they could return to their homelands. It did not present any difficulties as Transall planes and DC3s were at the ready for takeoff.

Overall, the mission had been carried out successfully.

Georges was briefed by Lefort about my health status and was very happy. In the bus on the way to base camp, I asked Lefort about my injury and the doctor. "Captain, what happened back there in the hut when I got wounded and who was that doctor?"

Lefort explained that the convoy had been in dire straits with rebels and Simbas attacking from all sides. Those covering me were killed even before I had reached the hut. He heard my two shots, and when I did not come out of the hut, he knew that something was very wrong. He and two British legionnaires went to find me and saw me wounded on the floor with the two dead Simbas by my side. They never saw any trace of the Red Cross nurse, who had probably been kidnapped by the Simbas weeks prior to our intervention. Lefort had understood that I was definitely dying. I was comatose with a very weak pulse and incoherent with pain.

He continued his story. "Suddenly a very tall doctor barged in with three Asian nurses carrying small black briefcases. He was blond, with a Red Cross badge around his neck, and they were all dressed in white. I had never seen him before. He spoke English with an American accent, but the nurses never said a word. They had strange eyes, very black, and they were very short in stature. He gave me his name, it was Jameson.

"My English is not good, so one of the British legionnaires translated what he was saying: You were dying, your heartbeat was almost indiscernible and the arrow had pierced your liver. Immediate surgery was required and he could do it. It was a matter of minutes before you died. He also told me that he was a specialist of internal medicine at the best hospital in Boston and that he was new in Africa working for the Red Cross. His team was from Hong Kong.

"I told him to operate and do what had to be done.

"He insisted on complete privacy, so I placed two men outside the hut to guard the door. I was not very optimistic for the outcome of this surgery because I had not noticed any equipment, the hut was totally unsanitary and we had no blood for transfusion. But there was no other solution. I even thought of using one of the helicopters to evacuate you, but it would not have helped, you were almost dead.

"There were no hospitals in the area. Stanleyville was out of the question. The Simbas and rebels were hammering us and you only had a few minutes to live. The apparition of Doctor Jameson was a miracle and even though I did not think that he could save you in such primitive conditions, I had to let him try, no matter what. Did I have any other choice?"

"What about the Simbas and the rebels?" I asked.

"You know, that was another strange occurrence. All of a sudden the sky blackened and in a matter of minutes a storm developed. The area became as dark as night. The rain started to pour and it was so heavy that it reminded me of the monsoon in Vietnam. I had never seen anything like this in the Congo, never."

"What happened next?" I inquired.

"Well, the fighting stopped almost immediately. The Simbas ran away. I gathered my men together and kept the buses safe and under cover. Because the helicopters could not fly in such weather, I grounded them, positioning them to protect the hut and the foreigners with their machine guns. I sent a reconnaissance patrol to look for warriors and they returned with good news. The Simbas had fled, scared to death. We were all safe to make for the airport to return home."

Lefort looked out of the bus window, puzzled, shaking his head. I could see that he had been really bothered by these events.

"What's troubling you, Captain?" I asked.

"I'm a soldier. I've dealt with the worst possible situations in my military career. Over the years, I've encountered very tough and strange circumstances. But today tops it all. It's totally inexplicable!"

"Why, Captain?" I inquired.

"I cannot stop thinking about the correlation between Dr Jameson and his team and the sudden and inexplicable change in the weather. It all happened at the same time. Do you understand?" Lefort replied, with a grimace.

I knew and understood Lefort's frustration, but all I could do was to agree and sympathize with him. He would never figure it all out.

Father Lapineau had listened to our conversation. Now he turned around to face Lefort and said, "Captain, I hate to use a cliché, but God works in mysterious ways, so why try to understand this mysterious occurrence? You will not be able to. God performed wonderful deeds today and saved us all. Accept them with grace. It was fate, definitely not luck. If this young man was resuscitated by the Lord and survives, it is because it was not his time to die. The Lord decides our fate, not ourselves, nor the enemy.

"Of course, Lefort," Father Lapineau continued, "You could ask yourself, was Jameson Jesus himself? Were the nurses his angels? Did God turn the weather around to get rid of the Simbas? Did Jesus prevent a massacre today?

"You could make all the assumptions that you want, Lefort, revolving what has happened, around and around in your mind, but you will never know the real truth, so why don't you accept this! After all, you are a realistic man, a man of action and a soldier. As a Jesuit priest, I have observed my share of mysteries and have accepted them as the work of the Lord. The church calls them miracles, revelations or supernatural phenomena. I use the words, 'the work of the Lord'.

"Our destiny is mapped out ahead of time, and sometimes it is not all we have hoped for. At other times it is more than we expected. In any case, it's all decided for us, God makes all the decisions.

"Look, we all survived this ordeal. I am very saddened that you have lost a lot of good men in this operation. But they were soldiers who knew the risks of war. They fought bravely to protect us, but did not survive because the Lord had other plans for them. In our eyes they were our saviours and be assured that I will pray for them.

"You have brought back safely two buses full of evacuees. You will be hailed as a hero. You will be a very famous French army officer. Mission accomplished, Lefort! Let's move on and be thankful that God was with us today!"

Then Father Lapineau looked at me again, smiling, gave me another wink, and closed his eyes.

All the passengers on the bus had listened to his speech and when he stopped they all applauded loudly and began to pray.

Lefort nodded his head thoughtfully, but I could see in his eyes that he had not been convinced by the priest's eloquence.

"Lefort, may I ask you another question?" I inquired.

"Shoot!" he replied.

"How long did the surgery last?"

"That's another mystery. No more than thirty minutes. Such an operation would have required at least two or three hours under the best of conditions in a modern hospital. But this took place in an African hut, with no running water, no electricity, no surgical tools that I could see, and surrounded by the worst sanitary elements imaginable. It is a miracle that you survived at all and oddly enough without any trace of infection.

"You see, this tall doctor barged in on us from out of nowhere with a team of tiny nurses, cut you open, and sewed you back up in half an hour. Then they simply evaporated into thin air? No, I don't buy it, it's too weird! Can you at least help me on that?" he questioned.

"No I can't help you, because I was out, unconscious. I don't even remember a doctor called Dr Jameson. I only woke up when you came into the hut. I recall being hit by the arrow, but after that it's all a blank."

Lefort was slowly caressing his chin, looking perplexed.

"Captain," I asked him, "the doctor wanted complete privacy and did not want anyone to intrude during the surgery, correct?"

"Yes."

"So, why did you come into the hut?" I asked.

Lefort did not reply, he was avoiding my eye and clearing his throat.

"Captain, answer me," I insisted.

"If I tell you, you won't believe me," he whispered. He looked at the window and seemed dazed and confused.

"Try me," I said.

"No, it's too crazy, I can't," he mumbled.

"A voice spoke to you, Lefort, didn't it?" interjected Father Lapineau. He had woken up and was looking intensely at the captain. "A voice repeatedly requested that you go and fetch the soldier who had been saved. Am I correct, Captain?" he questioned.

Lefort answered: "Yes, you are right, Father, this very deep voice kept saying over and over again, 'He's saved, he's saved. Go and get him out of the hut.' I didn't know where it was coming from, but I went to get him out anyway."

The captain seemed embarrassed by this declaration, but Father Lapineau reassured him: "You did the right thing, Lefort. We are all on our way home safely. You should never question the ways of the Lord! He does his thing, we do ours. Am I making sense, Captain?"

"Yes, Father, but it's sometimes very difficult to swallow," retorted Lefort.

Father Lapineau smiled gently and went back to sleep.

"You know," Lefort said to me then. There was something very bizarre going on during your surgery, but I didn't witness what they did, as Dr Jameson forbad anyone to enter the hut,"

"What makes you say that, Captain?" I asked.

"About fifteen minutes after Dr Jameson had arrived I went to the hut. The Simbas had fled because of the storm. The two soldiers were guarding the perimeter. I could hear strange sounds coming from inside the hut, rumbling, whistling, and sparkling sounds. It was odd. Then we heard voices, speaking in a language we could not comprehend, and bird-like chirping noises." Lefort was grimmacing again. "Is there anything that you remember about the surgery?"

"No, Captain, I never even saw Dr Jameson and his nurses. I was comatose, you remember!"

"Sorry, I had to ask! I find it all very strange, you understand." He shrugged his shoulders and went to sit at the back of the bus.

***

Soon we arrived at Base Camp. All of us were relieved to be in the midst of French soldiers and UN Forces. But we saw that the final departure would be hectic.

Georges was really happy to see me alive and well. He had been concerned about my health and for a short while thought that I was going to die.

Lefort was busy checking on his men and the planning for the convoy to the airport.

Due to the unexpectedly large number of foreigners for evacuation, Mobutu had arranged for additional buses The group was so large that even jeeps and tanks were mobilized as means of transportation.

Georges and Lefort were very happy with the mission, since all foreigners had been accounted for and were now in safe hands. France had called in fighter planes as a precautionary measure to escort us to Paris and Nice.

When we left the camp it was still raining and there were no Simbas or militia in sight. We were ahead of schedule and the feeling of tension among the passengers had slowly dissipated. When we reached Stanleyville Airport two Transall planes were waiting on the tarmac flanked by three DC3s. All had their engines rolling, ready for takeoff.

I shook hands with Captain Lefort and in an emotional moment we stood hugging on the runway. He was going directly to Paris where many decorations were waiting for him. In my view he deserved every one of them.

I was flying to Nice Airport with Georges, really glad to be leaving the Congo.

When we landed in France, the media mobbed us, desperate for interviews and pictures. But Georges and I did not hang around. We drove away quickly to a local hospital where I stayed overnight for examination.

The doctors could not find anything wrong with me but were puzzled about the small scar on my right side. The following day I was transferred to the military hospital in Marseilles where I went through a battery of tests.

I had to repeat my story perhaps twenty times, including to five different medical officers. One of them, Chief Surgeon Colonel Garnier, was not very receptive.

I had been there for two days when Georges came to visit me. I was glad to see him and we talked about the mission a little more. It was still making headlines in the newspapers. Georges did not seem very concerned about this, as the coverage was all positive.

He informed me that Captain Lefort had received the *Legion d'Honneur* from the French president and had been promoted to the rank of commandant. This was great news! It brought tears to my eyes. I was so happy for Lefort. He was indeed a great officer.

Then Georges asked me about the surgery I had undergone in the hut. I had known that eventually he would bring it up and I did not mind. I told him the same story as I had told everyone – Lefort, the medical team in Nice, and all the doctors in Marseilles including Colonel Garnier.

This was that I could not remember anything because I was comatose and dying with an arrow through my liver. I had killed two Simba warriors. I recalled that moment but nothing after that. It was obvious that my small scar baffled everyone concerned, but there was nothing I could do about it.

When I finished, Georges looked at me with a pensive expression on his face. He cleared his throat and gave me a very thick envelope.

"What's this?" I asked him.

"The other half of your pay, plus a risk and injury bonus."

I looked inside and could not believe my eyes. "Georges, this is a lot of money, are you sure?"

"Very much so. You deserve every penny of it." Then he said, "You know, the colonel called the Boston General Hospital in the United States and they've never heard of a Dr Jameson with a Chinese team. Neither have the Red Cross. They checked other major hospitals across America: no Dr Jameson. What do you think about that?" asked Georges.

"I do not think anything, Georges. I was almost dead and never saw Dr Jameson and his team. Lefort woke me up and when he did, I was fine. Strange, but true!" Georges nodded and smiled.

"Okay, I'll leave you now. Is there anything else that you need?"

"Yes there is, Georges! Get me out of here! There is nothing else that I can tell them, the colonel does not like me and I want to leave and return to my job."

"Fine, I'll do that for you and I'll see you soon in Monaco. Take care!" And with that, Georges left.

A few hours later I was released from the hospital and went to visit my family in Aix-en-Provence. Because of the reports in the press, my parents knew the entire story – or most of it – and were very upset, but it had been my choice to participate in this rescue and I felt proud of it.

Now I was ready to get back to work and prepare myself for the next big move: going to England to work at a five star hotel and learn English fluently to pursue my career.

Throughout the summer season I worked at the Hôtel de Paris in Monte Carlo and left for London in October.

Before moving to England I went to see Georges at the bar in Monaco and he told me, "Lefort spoke very highly of you the last time he called me and he suggested that you re-enlist in the Army. You could keep your rank of sergeant and he recommended a paratroop regiment in which you would fit perfectly. What do you think about this?"

"Tell Lefort, 'Thank you, but no thanks!'" I replied.

We said our goodbyes and I took the train to Aix-en-Provence to visit my family once more.

I went to visit my father at the Hôtel du Roy René, and he presented me with a letter. "An old Jesuit priest came during the night last week and left it for you with the night porter. It's very rare to see them at a hotel. Do you know him?" asked my father.

I shrugged my shoulders and opened the letter.

To Sergeant Gerard Breissan,

Take good care of yourself. Stay the way you are but pray more. You know now that miracles occur but you must clear the path for them. The Devil will block them, so you must free the passages through Prayer.

Perhaps one day, we'll meet again on Toki.

Don't forget to take a raincoat. London is wet!

Best wishes for the future.

*   – Father Lapineau*

My Dad looked at me and said: "What's wrong, Son? You are so white and look puzzled all of a sudden! Bad news?"

"No, Dad, but it's very weird. This Jesuit is more than a priest. He's a special person. He knows the future and a great deal about me. He talks about miracles. I don't know why he's interested in me." I shook my head.

"Have you met him before?"

I told my dad about Africa and the circumstances of my meeting Father Lapineau when I was working for the evacuation of foreigners from the Congo.

"Strange things occur in those lands, Son, and yes miracles happen all the time, they do exist, you are a product of a miracle yourself. As your father, I can recall a few times when you have escaped death. They were very close calls, including when you were born. The Lord was with you that day. Just now in Africa, you were badly hurt, and the media reports said that you would be dead if an American surgeon hadn't pulled out that arrow.

"What do you think, Son?" my dad asked. Were these miracles or not?"

"You are right, Dad. Father Lapineau is right too. Miracles do take place and we should let the Lord do his work and accept the way he's doing it.

"Africa opened my eyes. It was a beneficial experience for me even though I almost lost my life there. I am glad that I met Father Lapineau and I enjoyed his wisdom."

"What name did you say?" questioned my dad.

"Father Lapineau."

"Mmmmm! That's quite a coincidence," said my father touching his chin.

"What's that, Dad?"

"When I was a young kid," he answered, "I was an altar boy at St Sauveur Basilica here in town. One day a new priest took over the parish. He was very old, perhaps in his late 70s, maybe early 80s. The congregation loved him. He was still very strong and healthy for his age. His name was Father Lapineau. He preached powerful sermons on Sundays. He was never late for service, helped the poor, and taught us catechism every Thursday evening.

"He was not a local man and told us that he had come from a place far away. We never understood what he meant by that."

"Do you remember the name of the place, Dad?"

"A strange single word like Topi, Tobi, Toki, something like that."

"Toki, Dad?"

"Yes, that's it! It was Toki, I remember," my Dad said. "Actually, we tried to look it up in the dictionary but could not find the word Toki, so we just forgot about it. He worked at St Sauveur Basilica for many years. Then one day he just left the church and we never saw him again. But you know, Son, it can't be the same man."

"Why is that, Dad?"

"I was ten years of age when I first knew him and he was already seventy or eighty years old. That would make him almost a hundred and twenty-five years old now!"

We looked at each other silently and nodded.

I looked at the lobby's glass door and I knew without doubt that it was the same man. Eudoxus had told me that people on Toki were ageless. Father Lapineau had appeared in my life purposefully, sent by Eudoxus, first through my father. Then he had followed me through my life up to now, guarding me, watching me, protecting me and saving my skin when it was necessary. The two of them had watched over me since I was born. There was no coincidence there at all.

"What are you thinking about, Son?" my father asked.

"You know, Dad... Father Lapineau...this letter you gave me...your story...miracles which occurred...my stint as a mercenary in Africa and being wounded. It's all very remarkable and odd at the same time. I don't know what to make of it, really."

"Don't think about it too much, Son," my dad replied. "Take things in your stride and relax. Concentrate now on learning English. Focus your energy on the present, not the past. I remember Father Lapineau telling us, the Lord works in mysterious ways. Do not fight it, accept it, be patient and let it be. Things will always fall into place if you give them time. He was right, Son. And look, it has worked well for you, hasn't it?"

"He told me the same thing back in Africa, Dad," I told him.

My father smiled, nodded in agreement and hugged me tight. I left the hotel and felt the urge to pray.

I went to St Sauveur Cathedral before flying to England.

Soon, I was working at the Savoy Hotel in London. To this day it is one of the best hotels in the world.

In England I trained and studied full time building up a strong base and planned a successful career in the hospitality industry.

I loved the country and its people, it was a wonderful experience and I felt safe because Eudoxus was looking out for me and protecting me against evil.

I was on my way up. I was twenty-one years old....

A NOTE ON THE NAME, "EUDOXUS"

Two ancient Greeks had the name Eudoxus or Eudoxos. One was
Eudoxus of Cnidus (c. 408 BC – c. 347 BC), an astronomer and
mathematician. One was Eudoxus of Cyzicus (fl. 130 BC),
Greek navigator.
A crater on the moon has been named Eudoxus and asteroid
11709 is also named Eudoxus.

SOME OBSERVATIONS BY THE AUTHOR,
REGARDING UFO SIGHTINGS WORLDWIDE

1.   Widespread reports of UFO sightings and a popular fear
of aliens seems to have begun in 1938, when Orson Welles made
a radio broadcast in the USA of an adaptation of H. G. Wells'
novel, "The War of the Worlds". The programme had an
immediate dramatic result. Listeners really believed that beings
from other planets were attacking Earth. It is arguable that the
long-term impact of this broadcast was to root in the popular
imagination the possibility that such an event really could
happen and at any time.
2.   Beginning in the mid 1940s some have claimed that the
1908 Tunguska explosion over the forest in Siberia in Russia was
caused by a UFO crashing to the ground.
3.   In the early 1950s the Belgian cartoonist Herge predicted
space flights through his work. The hero of his adventures, Tintin,
a young reporter, lands on the moon and experiences many
adventures. Herge was well ahead of his time!
4.   In 1965, a large, brilliant fireball was seen by thousands in
at least six US states and Ontario, Canada. Some claimed that an
object had crashed from the sky into the woods in Kecksberg,
Philadelphia. Suggestions as to its nature include the assertion that
it was a UFO landing.
5.   Some fifty years ago, several apparitions of
flying-saucers were reported in the South of France. The story
goes that a number of cows were taken on board some
spaceships and returned to the same location years later. When

examined by veterinarians on their return, it seemed that they had not aged and had become more productive.[1]

6.   In 1970 in the South of France, a physician dying of terminal cancer had very little time left to live. One evening while resting on his balcony, he was hit by a laser ray from a UFO which had landed on his property. Almost immediately he started to walk again and within forty-eight hours he was completely cured from his illness. His doctors called it a miracle.[2]

7.   In the early 1970s a man was abducted in his car by aliens while driving through the South of England. He was found dirty, disheveled and in a state of shock in Sao Paulo, at the wheel of his vehicle, without proper papers, no passport, no currency, no visa and no reason to be there. He could not even speak the language. It was such an incomprehensible story that both countries kept quiet about it and the man was returned home. The Englishman remembered nothing, only that he was driving home from work when he saw an enormous ball of fire on the highway in front of him and then... nothing....[3]

8.   In December 1980, a series of episodes of sightings of bright lights over Rendlesham, Forest, Suffolk, in England, were widely publicized in some media as UFO sightings and landings.

9.   The South of France is definitely a vortex for UFO sightings. It is an inspirational center, full of creativity, offering a high quality of life. There is a need for other civilizations to come, search and learn from this part of the world, so Eudoxus told me during our first encounter.

---

[1] I learned about this from contemporary newspapers, radio and TV, while living in Canada; also from major newspapers. Later, the stories were re-enacted and replayed on US TV shows in programmes discussing UFO sightings, etc. – *Author*

[2] The same.

[3] The same.

ABOUT PROVERSE HONG KONG

Proverse Hong Kong is based in Hong Kong with long-term and expanding regional and international connections.

Proverse has published novels, novellas, fictionalized autobiography, non-fiction (including autobiography, biography, history, memoirs, sport, travel narratives), single-author poetry collections, children's, teens / young adult and academic books. Other interests include diaries, and academic works in the humanities, social sciences, cultural studies, linguistics and education. Some Proverse books have accompanying audio texts. Some are translated into Chinese.

Proverse welcomes authors who have a story to tell, wisdom, perceptions or information to convey, a person they want to memorialize, a neglect they want to remedy, a record they want to correct, a strong interest that they want to share, skills they want to teach, and who consciously seek to make a contribution to society in an informative, interesting and well-written way. Proverse works with texts by non-native-speaker writers of English as well as by native English-speaking writers.

The name, "Proverse", combines the words "prose" and "verse" and is pronounced accordingly.

THE PROVERSE PRIZE

The Proverse Prize, an annual international competition for an unpublished book-length work of fiction, non-fiction, or poetry, was established in January 2008. It is open to all who are at least eighteen on the date they sign the entry form. Unusually for a competition of this nature, there is no restriction based on nationality, residence or citizenship.

The objectives of the Proverse Prize are: to encourage excellence and / or excellence and usefulness in publishable written work in the English Language, which can, in varying degrees, "delight and instruct". Entries are invited from anywhere in the world. Semi-finalists to date include writers born or resident in Andorra, Australia, Canada, Germany, Hong Kong, New Zealand, Nigeria, Singapore, South Africa, Taiwan, The Bahamas, the Peoples' Republic of China, the United Arab Emirates, the United Kingdom, the USA.

Founders: Verner Bickley and Gillian Bickley. To celebrate their lifelong love of words in all their forms as readers, writers, editors, academics, performers, and publishers.
Honorary Legal Advisor: Mr Raymond T. L. Tse.
Honorary Accountant: Mr Neville Chow.
Honorary Judges: Anonymous.
Honorary Advisors: Bahamian poet Marion Bethel; UK translator, Margaret Clarke; UK linguist & lexicographer David Crystal; Canadian poet and academic, Jonathan Hart; Swedish linguist Björn Jernudd; Hong Kong University Librarian, Peter Sidorko; Singapore poet Edwin Thumboo; Czech novelist & poet Olga Walló.
Honorary UK agent and distributor: Christine Penney
Honorary Administrators: Proverse Hong Kong.

Proverse Prize Winners Whose Books Have Already Been Published By Proverse Hong Kong

Laura Solomon, Rebecca Jane Tomasis, Gillian Jones,
David Diskin, Peter Gregoire, Sophronia Liu, Birgit Linder, James McCarthy, Celia Claase, Philip Chatting.

Summary Terms and Conditions
(for indication only & subject to revision)

The information below is for guidance only. Please refer to the year-specific Proverse Prize Entry Form & Terms & Conditions, which are uploaded in April each year onto the Proverse Hong Kong website: <www.proversepublishing.com>.

The free Proverse E-Newsletter includes ongoing information about the Proverse Prize. To be put on the E-Newsletter mailing-list, email: info@proversepublishing.com with your request.

The Prize
1) Publication by Proverse Hong Kong, with
2) Cash prize of HKD10,000 (HKD7.80 = approx. US$1.00)

Supplementary publication grants may be made to selected other entrants for publication by Proverse Hong Kong.

Depending on the quality of the work in any year, the prize may be shared by at most two entrants or withheld, as recommended by the judges.

In 2015, the entry fee was: HKD220.00 OR GBP32.00.

Writers are eligible, who are at least eighteen on the date they sign The Proverse Prize entry documents. There is no nationality or residence restriction.

Each submitted work must be an unpublished publishable single-author work of non-fiction, fiction or poetry, the original work of the entrant, and submitted in the English language. School textbooks and plays are ineligible.

Translated work: If the work entered is a translation from a language other than English, both the original work and the translation should be previously unpublished. The submitted work will not be judged as a translation but as an original work.

Extent of the Manuscript: within the range of what is usual for the genre of the work submitted. However, it is advisable that novellas be in the range 30,000 to 45,000 words); other fiction (e.g. novels, short-story collections) and non-fiction (e.g. autobiographies, biographies, diaries, letters, memoirs, essay collections, etc.) should be in the range, 75,000 to 100,000 words. Poetry collections should be in the range, 5,000 to 25,000 words. Other word-counts and mixed-genre submissions are not ruled out.

Writers may choose, if they wish, to obtain the services of an Editor in presenting their work, and should acknowledge this help and the nature and extent of this help in the Entry Form.

KEY DATES FOR THE PROVERSE PRIZE
IN ANY YEAR
(subject to confirmation and/or change)

Receipt of Entry Fees / Entry Documents	Variable but no later than14 April to 31 May
Receipt of entered manuscripts	1 May to 30 June
Announcement of semi-finalists	July-September
Announcement of finalists	October-December
Announcement of winner/ max two winners (sharing the cash prize)	December of the year of entry to April of the year that follows the year of entry
Cash Award made	At the same time as publication of the work(s) adjudged the winner / joint-winners of the Proverse Prize
Publication of winning work(s)	In or after November of the year that follows the year of entry

~~~~~~~~~~~~~~~

NOVELS, SHORT STORY COLLECTIONS
AND OTHER FICTION
Published by Proverse Hong Kong

A Misted Mirror, by Gillian Jones. 2011.
A Painted Moment, by Jennifer Ching. 2010.
An Imitation of Life, by Laura Solomon. 2013.
Article 109, by Peter Gregoire. 2012.
Bao Bao's Odyssey: from Mao's Shanghai to Capitalist Hong Kong, by Paul Ting. 2012.
Black Tortoise Winter, by Jan Pearson. Scheduled 2015 / 2016.
Bright Lights and White Nights, by Andrew Carter. 2015.
cemetery miss you, by Jason S Polley. 2011.
Cop Show Heaven, by Lawrence Gray. 2015.
Death has a Thousand Doors, by Patricia Grey. 2011.
Hilary and David, by Laura Solomon. 2011.
Instant Messages, by Laura Solomon. 2010.
Man's Last Song, by James Tam. 2013.
Mila the Magician, by Zhang Jian. 2013. (English / Chinese bilingual)
Mishpacha – Family, by Rebecca Tomasis. 2010.
Odds and Sods, by Lawrence Gray. 2013.
Paranoia (the Walk and Talk with Angela), by Caleb Kavon. 2012.
Red Bird Summer, by Jan Pearson. 2014.
Revenge from Beyond, by Dennis Wong. 2011.
The Day They Came, by Gérard Louis Breissan. 2012.
The Devil You know, by Peter Gregoire. 2014.
The Monkey in Me: Confusion, Love and Hope under a Chinese Sky, by Caleb Kavon. 2009.
The Monkey in Me, by Caleb Kavon. Translated by Chapman Chen. 2010. E-book. 2010. (Chinese)
The Perilous Passage of Princess Petunia Peasant, by Victor Edward Apps. 2014.
The Reluctant Terrorist: in Search of the Jizo, by Caleb Kavon. 2011.
The Shingle Bar Sea Monster and Other Stories, by Laura Solomon. 2012.
The Snow Bridge and Other Stories, by Philip Chatting. Scheduled 2015.

Tiger Autumn, by Jan Pearson. 2015.
The Village in the Mountains, by David Diskin. 2012.
Tightrope! A Bohemian Tale, by Olga Walló. Translated from Czech by Johanna Pokorny, Veronika Revická & others. 2010.
Tightrope! A Bohemian Tale, by Olga Walló. Translated by Chapman Chen. 2011. (Chinese)
University Days, by Laura Solomon. 2014.
Vera Magpie, by Laura Solomon. 2013.

OTHER GENRES

We also publish in other genres, including autobiography, biography, children's illustrated books, educational books, Hong Kong educational and legal history, memoirs, poetry, teenage / young adult books, and travel. Other genres may be added.

WRITE TO US!

We are interested to read your response to
Gerard Breissan's *The Day They Came*
and any other of our publications.
Please write to our email address, proverse@netvigator.com,
giving us a few sentences
which you are willing for us to publish,
giving your comments on this book.
If what you write is chosen to be included
in our E-Newsletter or website,
we will select another title published by Proverse
and send you a complimentary copy.
Please include your name, email address and mailing address
when you write to us, and state whether or not we may cut or
edit your comments for publication.
We will use your initials to attribute your comments.

FIND OUT MORE ABOUT OUR AUTHORS AND BOOKS

Visit our website
http://www.proversepublishing.com

Visit our distributor's website
<www.chineseupress.com>

Follow us on Twitter
Follow news and conversation: <twitter.com/Proversebooks>
OR
Copy and paste the following to your browser window and
follow the instructions: https://twitter.com/#!/ProverseBooks

'Like us' on **Facebook**: www.facebook.com/ProversePress

Request our E-Newsletter
Send your request to info@proversepublishing.com.

Availability
Most titles are available in Hong Kong and world-wide
from our Hong Kong based Distributor,
The Chinese University Press of Hong Kong,
The Chinese University of Hong Kong, Shatin, NT,
Hong Kong SAR, China. Email: cup-bus@cuhk.edu.hk

All titles are available from Proverse Hong Kong
and the Proverse Hong Kong UK-based Distributor.

We have stock-holding retailers in Hong Kong,
Singapore (Select Books), Canada (Elizabeth Campbell Books),
Principality of Andorra (Llibreria La Puça, La Llibreria).

Orders can be made from bookshops in the UK and elsewhere.

Ebooks
Most of our titles are available also as Ebooks.